# ARMOURON™

'Stand Together . . . Battle as One!'

**PRISONER ON KASTEESH**

The Armouron:
Don't miss any of the
titles in this awesome series:

## PRISONER ON KASTEESH

Richard Dungworth

BANTAM BOOKS

ARMOURON: PRISONER ON KASTEESH
A BANTAM BOOK 978 0 553 82197 0

First published in Great Britain by Bantam Books,
an imprint of Random House Children's Books
A Random House Group Company

Bantam edition published 2010

1 3 5 7 9 10 8 6 4 2

The Random House Group Limited supports the Forest Stewardship
Council (FSC), the leading international forest certification organization.
All our titles that are printed on Greenpeace-approved FSC-certified paper
carry the FSC logo. Our paper procurement policy can be found at
www.rbooks.co.uk/environment.

**Mixed Sources**
Product group from well-managed
forests and other controlled sources
www.fsc.org  Cert no. TT-COC-2139
© 1996 Forest Stewardship Council

Set in Palatino

Bantam Books are published by Random House Children's Books,
61–63 Uxbridge Road, London W5 5SA

www.**kids**atrandomhouse.co.uk
www.**rbooks**.co.uk

Addresses for companies within The Random House Group Limited
can be found at: www.randomhouse.co.uk/offices.htm

THE RANDOM HOUSE GROUP Limited Reg. No. 954009

A CIP catalogue record for this book is available from the British Library.

Printed in the UK by CPI Bookmarque, Croydon, CR0 4TD

Far back in the mists of time, an order of warrior knights was forged. They were the Armouron: a dozen heroes dedicated to the ideals of honour and justice. And twelve totems of great power, each borne in the breastplate of an Armouron's suit, were crafted by these First Knights.

The order grew steadily in strength and number. The knowledge, skills and experience of one generation of knights passed to the next.

For millennia, the Armouron campaigned against corruption. But the order came under threat. Giant corporations fought to seize the balance of galactic power. In the struggle to oppose them, all but a handful of Armouron were killed. The survivors were scattered across space.

Now the galaxy has fallen on dark days. Many worlds, including Earth, have been overrun by the largest of the power-hungry corporations. Perfect Corp, led by the sinister Chairman, controls every aspect of life on Earth.

Hope still burns, however, in the Armouron medallions. Many are lost. But five of the original Twelve have found their way into the hands of a group of youngsters, living in the city of Nu-Topia, at the very heart of the Chairman's corrupt regime.

A new generation of Armouron Knights . . .

# The new generation of the Armouron

## Rake
Armouron title: Templer, the Fearless
Role: Strategy and Offence

## Tea-Leaf
Armouron title: Balista, the Shadow
Role: Spy and Scout

## Oddball
Armouron title: Sappar, the Inventive
Role: Scavenger and Engineer

## Hoax
Armouron title: False-Light, the Trickster
Role: Deception and Misdirection

## Snow
Armouron title: Alida, the Shieldmaiden
Role: Protection and Evasion

## The Armouron master
## Salt

Armouron title: Claymore

Role: Master Craftsman and Teacher

## The Armouron Code:

Honour, Duty, Compassion and Justice

1. Perfect Corporation
2. Gladiator Arena
3. Salt's Workshop
4. Armouron Academy
5. Old School
6. SeeBlock Tower
7. Perfect Vision HQ
8. Nu-Topia Hospital
9. Shopping Mall
10. Peace Keeps
11. Fuel Dumps
12. The Park
13. Waste Dumps
14. Epsilon Power Station
15. Spaceport

SOLAR FURNACE FIELDS

THE BEACH

PV

NU-TOPIA

SMELTING PLANT

## Prologue

Parqul-Tuz extended his central eyestalk to take a closer look at the stranger standing before him. *Homo sapiens*, by the looks of him. An Earthling.

'You're a long way from home, human,' growled Tuz. He shifted his bulky body awkwardly in his air-chair. 'We don't get many of your kind in our part of the galaxy. What brings you to Auroxila, I wonder?'

The stranger held Tuz's suspicious three-eyed glare with his own intelligent gaze.

'I have been travelling for some time,' he said quietly.

'Hmph!' The Auroxilan gave a sceptical grunt. 'I'll bet you have! Another cheating scoundrel on the run, no doubt. So tell me – why should I be tempted to give you work, hmm?'

'I am strong and do not tire easily,' replied the man. 'If you hire me as a labourer, you will get good value for whatever credits you choose to pay me.'

Tuz gave another grunt. But he could see that the man wasn't boasting. He had met humans before and most were puny. This one looked tough. He wasn't tall, but he had a powerful, well-toned physique. His head-fur was unlike that of the other men Tuz had encountered, too – it was pure white.

'I should warn you,' said Tuz, 'I pride myself on paying badly. And a decent lifestyle on this Gomm-forsaken planet doesn't come cheap.'

'I do not intend to stay,' replied the man. 'That is why I seek work. I wish to earn my starship passage as soon as possible.'

'Heading back home to Earth, hmm?' probed Tuz.

A wistful look crossed the human's face.

It was ten years since the man had fled his birth planet. Ten years spent as a fugitive, always moving on, endlessly tormented by the memory of what he had left behind.

But not any more. He was tired of running from the Corporation. Let them do their worst. He would hide no longer.

Parqul-Tuz was impressed with the determination that burned in the human's eyes as he eventually replied.

'Yes,' said the stranger, quietly but firmly. 'I'm going back . . .'

# Chapter 1
## The Voice

Snow tried to calm her mind and focus. *Panic is your greatest enemy.* That was what Salt had told them. *Fear only clouds your senses.*

She kept her eyes fixed on the strange mechanical device hovering at eye level a few metres away. It was gunmetal-grey and the size and shape of a handball. It was moving erratically – left, right, up, down – kept airborne by a whirring rotor. Its lower surface bristled with tubular silver spines. She had no idea which of them would shoot. She was on the balls of her feet, knees slightly bent, ready to dodge.

There was a sudden *pfft* of escaping air. Snow threw herself into a dive to her left. Something fizzed past her to ricochet off the stone floor, kicking up a little puff of dust.

Snow used the momentum of her dive to roll through and spring back onto her feet. When the device fired its second shot an instant later, she was ready.

This time she sensed its aim was low. She launched herself into a high tuck-jump and another tiny projectile whistled past under her feet.

She landed lightly – in time to hear the device let out a third soft hiss. Snow ducked urgently to the right. But she was a fraction too slow.

There was a metallic *ping!* and Snow felt something glance off her armoured shoulder.

'Gotcha!'

Oddball stepped forward, grinning. He strode towards the spiky flying device. As it continued to dart about, he reached up to slap a switch on its underside. The machine's rotor immediately began to slow and it drifted lower. Oddball plucked it from the air. He turned to Snow, eyes sparkling behind his ever-present goggles.

'Two out of three – pretty impressive for a practice run!' he congratulated her.

He held up the peculiar flying device proudly.

'What do you make of it?'

Before Snow could answer, he went gabbling on.

'I thought I might call it the "PShooter". "P" for "pressure", you see, 'cos it runs entirely on compressed air. You just have to pump it up. The air chamber holds enough to power it for a couple of minutes. The shooter-tubes work off the same pressurized system. It's totally random which ones fire, of course – that's what keeps you on your toes!'

He gripped the gadget between his knees, produced a miniature hand pump and began energetically pumping air into a valve in the device's side.

'Salt asked me to put together something to help improve our reflexes. I thought this might do the job. I pinched the fan for the rotor from one of the big dryers in the laundry. The rest is just bits and bobs I found lying around.'

Snow watched him pumping away enthusiastically and smiled to herself. Every good team needed a techno-geek. Of the group of recently recruited Armouron Knights, Oddball was certainly that guy. Salt couldn't have found a more gadget-mad individual in the whole of the Academy – or Nu-Topia, for that matter.

*He must have had his reasons to choose each of us, I guess*, thought Snow.

It was several months now since Salt, the Academy's elderly armourer, had introduced Snow and her three fellow cadets – Oddball, Rake and Hoax – to an exciting new world of adventure and danger.

Up until then, their lives had been just like those of the other orphans raised at the Academy. Day in, day out, they had pursued their Gladiator training in preparation for their future careers in the Arena, where they would fight staged battles for the entertainment of Nu-Topia's citizens. They had been confined at all times to the Academy compound, kept within its walls like prisoners.

But not any more. Now, they lived double-lives. During the daytime, they continued as before, regular Academy cadets, attending their lessons and carrying out their chores. But by night, wearing the unique suits of armour that Salt had crafted for them, they became Alida, Sappar, Templer and False-Light, knights of the ancient order of the Armouron.

Salt had opened their eyes to the corruption in the world around them – the so-called 'Perfect World', as its unscrupulous ruler, the Chairman, called it. The Chairman had used his influence as leader of the all-powerful Corporation to brain-wash the citizens of Earth into believing his lies. Those who didn't were soon silenced by his sinister police force, the White Knights.

But under Salt's direction, Snow and her fellow

knights were fighting back – fighting to restore the ideals of their order: Honour, Duty, Compassion and Justice.

Not that they were in action every night. Most nights, like tonight, it was training. And more training. And then more training. Salt was a hard taskmaster. As an Armouron himself, he knew the value of being in peak physical and mental condition. He insisted that his young recruits were thoroughly drilled in the techniques and strategies of combat. Each night, down in the secret chambers of the Old School, beneath the Academy, he put them through their paces.

So far tonight, though, only Snow and Oddball were there for training.

They hadn't been expecting Tea-Leaf, the fifth member of the team. Unlike the others, Tea-Leaf wasn't an Academy cadet, but lived outside the compound, on the city streets. Her only route into the Old School was via a secret passage from the Academy's shuttle garage. Salt had heard news that the garage was to be under close police guard over the next few days. If White Knights were patrolling the area, it was better that Tea-Leaf stay well clear. During the previous night's session, he had warned her to stay away.

So a no-show from Tea-Leaf was no surprise. But Salt wasn't impressed when neither Hoax nor Rake turned up, either – even less so when Oddball confessed he had heard a rumour that the other boys were in a 'spot of bother'.

Salt had given a weary sigh, then departed to find out more – but not before instructing Oddball and Snow to work on their reaction times while he was gone.

Oddball suddenly detached the pump and pulled the PShooter from between his knees.

'That should do it!'

He lifted a flap in the gadget's casing, emptied a handful of small ball-bearings into it, then closed the flap again.

'OK – so this time is for real. Fully charged, she'll fire eight shots. We'll score how many you dodge. Rake managed five last night – that's the best so far.'

*Rake would like that*, thought Snow. It was pretty important to Rake to be the best at things. He liked to be in charge too. It didn't bother Snow – Rake made a pretty natural team-leader. But she knew it got on Hoax's nerves sometimes.

Tea-Leaf, too, didn't always take kindly to being told what to do.

'Are you ready?' asked Oddball, preparing to launch the PShooter.

But before Snow's trial could begin, a burly figure came limping along the passageway that led to the secret doorway back into the armoury. It was Salt. His expression was even more gruff than usual.

'What's he done this time, master?' asked Oddball. Hoax had a well-deserved reputation for mischief.

Salt gave a grunt of exasperation.

'Your young friend was apparently responsible for this evening's security alarm,' he growled. 'He seems to have believed – foolishly – that it would be amusing to stage a fake cadet breakout. From what I can gather, he got hold of a spare identity belt, yet to be registered, and put it down the canteen rubbish chute. When the refuse collection vehicle picked up the Academy's waste just after lights-out, it took the belt with it. Naturally, it triggered the security systems as it left the compound.'

Oddball tried to hide his smirk. 'And they

managed to pin it on Hoax, did they?' he said. 'It's not like him to get caught.'

'By all accounts, he was unable to contain his delight when his childish prank proved a success,' Salt explained, stony-faced. 'Supervisor Brand deduced from his mirth that he was responsible – despite Rake protesting there was no proof. Rake should have known better. Brand has given them both an overnight punishment detail.'

The old man suddenly clapped his bear-sized hands together.

'But enough of their foolishness! Let's get back to work!' He turned to Snow. 'How are those reaction times coming on, Alida?' he asked, using Snow's secret Armouron name.

'She's good,' answered Oddball on Snow's behalf. 'Really good. You should see some of her dodge moves!'

'I'm glad to hear it,' rumbled Salt. 'The armour I crafted for you, Alida, was specifically designed to enhance your natural agility. Only Balista's suit is lighter. It should allow you ease of movement, at all times.'

It was true. Snow still found it amazing that

wearing her blue armour made her *more* agile, not less. Any ordinary suit would have slowed you down. But there was nothing ordinary about the suits Salt had made for them.

'And remember,' continued Salt, 'your armour's evasive properties will be maximized only if you harness the power of your medallion. Connect to its Flow and your agility will be greatly increased.'

Snow raised a hand over her Armouron medallion, embedded in her breastplate, and nodded silently.

That concluded Salt's pep talk. He took a few steps backwards, to give Snow some space.

'Whenever you're ready then, Alida. Let's see what you can do.'

As Oddball got ready once more to release the PShooter, Snow prepared herself again, up on her toes, mind fully focused.

The device whirred into the air and immediately began darting from side to side.

Its first shot was aimed low, at Snow's legs. Snow side-stepped it easily. As the device released its next two missiles, almost simultaneously, she cartwheeled to the left. Both ball-bearings whistled harmlessly past. A swift dive and roll enabled her to dodge shots four and five. She was back on her feet in time to evade the device's next effort, then jump high to avoid another low-flying shot.

Eight shots, Oddball had said. That left just one more.

Suddenly, Snow's concentration was shattered by a nerve-splitting scream of anguish, which exploded in her mind.

She dropped helplessly to her knees and began clawing at her helmet clasp, as though releasing it might somehow let the agonizing yell out of her head.

Then, as abruptly as it had come, the tormenting cry of the mind-voice ceased.

Snow knelt on the stone floor, her body sagging. She had managed to tug her helmet off at last, but echoes of the voice were still resounding in her head.

Somewhere in the back of her throbbing mind, a part of Snow's brain registered the quiet hiss of the PShooter's final shot. But she was unable to move, still numb with shock. As the tiny missile rocketed straight towards her unprotected skull, she subconsciously willed it not to strike her.

At the last instant, the ball-bearing veered off-target and struck the floor behind her.

Snow was about to slump forward when strong hands grasped her shoulders. She looked up shakily to meet Salt's anxious gaze.

'Alida? Are you all right, Alida? . . . Snow?'

Oddball was standing behind Salt, looking at Snow with a mixture of concern and bewilderment.

'But . . . that last shot . . .' he murmured. 'She didn't dodge it . . . *It* dodged *her* . . .'

'Not now, Sappar,' said Salt firmly. He looked into Snow's face with evident concern. 'What happened, Alida?'

Snow shook her head, as if trying to clear it.

'I don't know,' she answered weakly. 'A pain. In my head. It's gone now.'

'Are you sure?'

'Yes. I'm . . . I'm OK . . .'

Salt cradled her chin in one of his massive, rough hands and looked directly into her eyes.

'Has anything like this happened before?'

Snow didn't answer immediately.

'No.' She shook her head feebly. 'No, this is the first time. I'm fine now. Really.'

With Salt's help, she got slowly to her feet.

The old armourer gave a low grunt. 'That's enough for tonight.' He turned to Oddball. 'Sappar, please help Alida remove and store her armour and see her safely back to her dormitory. We'll continue tomorrow.'

Salt gave Snow one last searching look, then turned and hobbled away.

'I don't get it,' muttered Oddball, as he undid the magna-buckle on Snow's left arm-guard. 'How can a ball-bearing going at that speed swerve off course?'

But Snow only shrugged weakly. Her mind was still spinning.

She hadn't told Salt the truth. She *had* heard the voice in her head before. In fact, it had been a recurring feature of her dreams over the last few nights. But on those occasions, it had been a faint cry, too quiet for her to make out what the voice was screaming.

But not this time. This time the single word that the voice was crying, with such anguish, had been all too clear.

*Hoshiko.*
A name.
A name she knew.
The name of her dead father.

## Chapter 2
### Mystery Cargo

Snow wasn't herself the next day. By the afternoon, even Rake had noticed that she was quieter than usual. And for Snow, that was saying something.

'Are you OK?'

The two cadets stood beside one another at one of the heavy benches of the Academy's armour workshop. They had both been assigned an afternoon of 'spit-'n'-polish' duty. On the benchtop before them lay several complete sets of Gladiator kit, awaiting cleaning. The flashy Arena gear didn't compare with their own Armouron suits.

Snow returned Rake's concerned look with an unconvincing smile.

'Yes. I'm fine. Just a bit tired.'

She applied a little more resin to her polishing cloth and continued silently rubbing away at the glossy red surface of a small round shield.

Rake tried again.

'Oddball told me about last night's training. Why do you think you collapsed?'

'It was just a bad headache, I think,' replied Snow softly. 'I'm fine, now. Really.'

Rake raised his eyebrows, but decided to let it go. He gave a sudden wide yawn, then put down the helmet he was polishing and stretched wearily.

'I'm pretty shattered myself. Thanks to Hoax,' he added grumpily. 'Brand worked us nearly all night. It wasn't even me who set the clacking alarm off!'

'I trust you have both now learned your lesson,' growled a deep voice. The cadets turned to find Salt in the doorway. 'Though in your friend's case at least, I doubt that very much.'

Rake gave his stern old mentor an uncomfortable smile.

'I have need of your assistance in the main storeroom, Rake,' Salt continued. 'We've just taken delivery of a new batch of armoury supplies. I'd like you to help me sort through them, please.' He turned to Snow. 'Can you manage the rest of these yourself, young lady?'

Snow nodded.

'See you at tea, then,' said Rake. He dropped his cloth onto the benchtop and followed Salt out into the passageway.

As soon as they had gone, Snow put down her own cloth. She massaged the sides of her forehead with her fingertips. She was only too glad to be left alone. Her mind was still echoing with last night's screaming voice. She had been finding it impossible to give proper attention to anything, or anyone, else.

She hadn't known how to tell Rake about the voice. Hearing things wasn't something you felt comfortable owning up to. It had been bad enough that her sleep had been so frequently disturbed recently. But hearing the voice when she was wide awake took things to a whole new level of weird.

It was funny, really. After wishing for so long that her bad dreams would stop, she now desperately wanted to hear the voice again. She had persuaded herself that she couldn't have heard her father's name last night – it didn't make any sense. She knew both her parents had died before she was even a year old. But she couldn't suppress a desire to hear the voice clearly again, just so she could be sure.

For the umpteenth time, she closed her eyes and tried to calm her thoughts. She hoped to bring the part of her brain in which the voice was still faintly echoing into focus.

But it was no good.

What had made it so clear last night?

A thought suddenly struck her. She had been wearing her Armouron suit, with her medallion in its breastplate. Salt had often impressed on the young knights the unique powers of the ancient totems. Perhaps it was her medallion that had amplified the voice so powerfully? Maybe it had something to do with the Flow – the heightened sense of awareness and responsiveness that each medallion gave its bearer?

There was only one way to find out.

Snow hurried to the tall toolrack that stood against the workshop's opposite wall. Salt and Rake would be busy in the storeroom for the rest of the afternoon. There was plenty of time for her to slip into the Old School, see if her medallion made any difference and still get the rest of the armour polished before evening mealtime.

She scanned the rack of spanners. She wanted . . . *that one*. She reached for the heavy tool and pulled it towards her. It slid forward, but didn't come free. Snow carefully rotated the spanner one full clockwise turn, then pushed it back into place.

A moment later, the toolrack swung silently out towards her. Behind it lay the opening of a passageway. Snow hurried through, into the secret chambers of the Old School beyond. The toolrack moved smoothly back into place.

She headed straight for the armour store, an annexe off the main training chamber. On its ancient stone wall, in a neat row, hung the five unique sets of armour, with their accompanying weapons, that Salt had crafted for his young Armouron recruits.

Snow's blue suit was by far the smallest. She lifted it down and carried it out into the training hall.

Now that she was about to try the medallion,

she was more than a little nervous about what the result might be. Last night, she had almost passed out. What if that happened again?

Trying not to lose her nerve, she pulled the medallion from its snap-grab housing in the centre of the breastplate. She put the armour aside and clutched the medallion tightly in her small right hand. Then she closed her eyes and once more tried to summon the voice in her mind.

She felt the familiar tingling sensation spread through her nervous system as she connected with the medallion's Flow.

Several seconds passed.

Then several more.

Nothing happened.

Snow felt her hopes draining away. Then another thought struck her. She had been wearing her helmet last night. Maybe *that* had had an effect, somehow.

She hurried back to the armour store, grabbed her helmet and put it on.

The effect was immediate and overwhelming.

*Hoshiko!*

Snow reeled against the wall, as the anguished cry filled her head once more. Leaning against its cold stones, she fought desperately to stay on her feet. She struggled to control her breathing and steady her racing pulse.

*Hoshiko!* wailed the voice again. *I am here!*

In a way that she could only feel, not understand, Snow had a vague sense of the voice's source. The mind-cry was coming from a particular direction, a particular place. And Snow's entire being compelled her to answer its call.

Drawn by an instinct she could not resist, Snow slowly and unsteadily made her way out of the storeroom and towards the hidden passage that led to the Academy shuttle garage. She stumbled along it, still wearing her helmet and clutching her medallion. Her mind throbbed with the echoes of the voice's last cry.

Snow reached the wall at the end of the passageway. She ran the fingers of her left hand along the mortar line above the third course of stones, at knee height, until she found a small gap. She eased her fingertips into it and released the catch inside. The entire section of wall swung silently towards her, creating an opening just wide enough for a person to pass. Snow slipped through, and the secret doorway closed behind her.

Even in her dazed state, Snow knew better than to wander aimlessly out into the main garage area. Supply shuttles ran frequently to and from the Academy and there was always a chance the garage would be occupied by technicians or cadets on loading duty. She mustn't be seen.

This afternoon, the garage was busier than usual. Snow ducked down behind a pallet of gruel-mix destined for the canteen kitchens, and peered out cautiously to see what all the activity was about.

There was only one vehicle currently occupying the garage. But it was large enough to take up most of the available space – much larger than the shuttles that typically docked there. It was a freight shuttle. Its rear cargo doors stood open, revealing its spacious hold within.

A pair of armed White Knights were patrolling the area around the shuttle's loading ramp. On its starboard side, facing her, Snow could see a large Perfect Corporation logo. Now she remembered Salt's warning to Tea-Leaf – about steering clear of the garage for a while.

The area between the freight shuttle and the supply stacks Snow was hiding behind was

occupied by a huge white cargo pod. It was in its collapsed state, for loading. Its four sides and top were folded down on their hinged edges so that the whole thing lay on the garage floor like a vast flat-plan. Two men were busy using mag-lev pallet-floats to manoeuvre a giant yellow canister, ten metres square, into the centre of the collapsed pod.

Snow recognized the overweight, balding man. He was the garage manager, one of the Academy staff. Judging by the other man's Corporation overalls, he was probably the shuttle's pilot.

From her hiding place, Snow eavesdropped on the conversation they were having.

'What's in the can, then?' the manager asked.

'Not sure. It's all a bit hush-hush,' said the pilot. 'I don't always get to know what I'm carrying – just fly where I'm told, no questions asked.' He nodded his head discreetly at the patrolling White Knights. 'But whatever it is, it's had an escort from the moment I picked it up.'

He lowered his voice, so that Snow had to strain to hear.

'From what I can gather, whatever is inside was meant to be the main event at the next big Gladiator show – something special for the beast-fight fans, I reckon. It's been shipped halfway across the galaxy, I know that much.'

The garage manager looked impressed, then a little puzzled.

'So how come we're loading it up again?' he asked quietly. 'Why didn't it make it into the Arena?'

'I overheard one of the guards saying that whatever it is, it's sick,' explained the pilot. 'Not fit to fight. So they're shipping it back to where it came from. Once you and I have got it safely loaded, I'm to shuttle it straight to the spaceport. There's a Corporation carrier ship being prepped for lift-off later today.'

'Can't say I'll be sorry to see you go,' admitted the garage manager. He cast an uneasy look in the direction of the White Knights. 'Having police crawling all over the place makes me edgy. I like to run my own shop.'

By now, the two men had dragged the huge yellow canister into position in the centre of the cargo pod's base. They powered down their pallet-floats and the canister settled gently to the floor. Both men stepped clear of the flattened pod.

'Right,' said the manager, taking a small remote from his toolbelt. 'Let's get her closed up.'

He pressed one of the remote's buttons. The sides of the cargo pod immediately began to fold up from the floor. The lid section, too, began to flap smoothly over, until . . .

*Bang!*

A puff of dark smoke and a shower of sparks suddenly burst from one of the pod's lower edges. It froze, with its transformation into a box-shape not quite complete.

'Dunk!' The manager gave the part-closed

pod a kick. 'These new PackSmith power hinges are clacking useless! I've had three blow in the last month! I'll have to fetch a spare. Give me a hand.'

He strode away, grumbling, to fetch the necessary part from his workshop. The pilot accompanied him.

Snow's gaze remained glued on the cargo pod. The weird mental pull she had first felt back in the armour store was drawing her towards the yellow canister. Somehow, she felt sure that the mysterious mind-call had come from something inside it.

*Hoshiko! Come!*

The cry came again, stronger and clearer, leaving her in no doubt about its source.

Snow watched the two White Knight sentries pacing back and forth. *If I can just get over there without those Kettles spotting me . . .*

She timed her dash for the moment both White Knights were turning, their backs momentarily towards her. She made it to the pod and squeezed her slight body through the narrow gap between two of its jammed side panels.

Once safely inside the pod, she took a good look

✖ ❦ ⟁ ◉ ⟐ Ⓐ ⟠ ◈ ◯ ✦

at the yellow canister. Up close, it seemed even bigger. It was at least three times Snow's height. Its sides were solid and sealed – there was no way to tell what they contained.

*Maybe there's an opening in the top,* thought Snow. *I might get a look inside from there . . .*

She slipped her medallion into her tunic pocket, and began to clamber agilely up the canister's ridged side.

She was two thirds of the way up when the mind-cry hit her again.

This time, its intensity was too great for Snow to bear. As her mind filled with the desperate yell of anguish, she clasped her hands to her helmet – and fell.

She hit the floor of the cargo pod hard and knew no more.

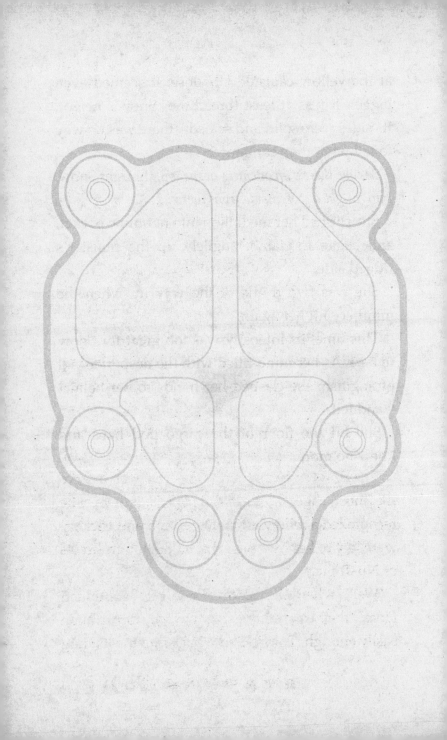

## Chapter 3
### Snow Alert

'Honestly, Tea-Leaf, it was *classic!*' bragged Hoax. 'When I shoved the ID-belt in the trash, I had no idea things would turn out so well. I was just hoping a fake alarm would stir the supervisors up a bit, maybe buy us a break from chores.' He grinned broadly. 'But it was *way* better than that!'

'Why? What happened?' Tea-Leaf was always the most eager admirer of Hoax's pranks. She recognized a fellow artist. Deception and trickery were key to her own survival on the tough streets of Nu-Topia.

'Well, when the alarm went off,' continued Hoax, 'they tracked the signal to the slops wagon easily enough. They called it back into the loading bay. Pretty soon there were supervisors all over it. Rake and I were on packing duty, so we got to watch.'

He chortled to himself.

'Picture the scene. By now, some of the Gladiators are helping out with the search. Our fat-headed friend Stamper is one of them. When they figure out that the signal is coming from inside the wagon's load chamber, he goes marching up to its main hatch, bold as brass, and wrenches it open to get at whoever is in there. And the slops wagon dumps pretty much its entire load right on top of him!'

He doubled up with laughter, delighting once again in Stamper's humiliation.

'It couldn't believe it,' he said, wiping his eyes. 'I nearly died!'

Rake was listening to his friend's account too. He looked anything but amused.

'What Mr Comedy here hasn't told you,' he said bitterly, 'is that after *he* played his oh-so-hilarious prank and then completely gave the game away, *we* spent most of last night clearing up the mess.'

'Yeah, sorry about that, mate,' said Hoax, looking not very sorry at all. 'And thanks for sticking up for me. "Stand Together" and all that . . .'

Rake snorted. 'I'm pretty sure that the Armouron founders didn't intend their code of honour to be interpreted as "cover up for your dunk-head friend". Still' – his scowl gave way to a sly grin – 'it *was* pretty sweet seeing Stamper standing there up to his neck in rubbish. Worth a few hours shovelling slops, I guess.'

Tea-Leaf laughed heartily. 'Nice one, Hoax! That muscle-bound bully deserves all the humiliation you can dish up!'

'Salt wasn't impressed when you two missed training, though,' said Oddball. He too was waiting in the Old School chamber. It was late evening, time for the young knights' next session of secret instruction with their Armouron mentor.

Tonight, it had proved safe for Tea-Leaf to join them. The large freight shuttle that had been so heavily guarded by White Knights over the past few days was no longer parked in the garage. Its police guard appeared to have left with it.

'The old man won't be too chuffed with Snow, either, if she doesn't turn up soon,' said Tea-Leaf.

As yet, there was no sign of the team's other female member. 'We ought to be getting our gear on in a few minutes. Where's she got to?'

'That, Balista,' growled a low voice, 'is a matter of some concern.'

The four youngsters turned to find Salt behind them. For a big man with a dodgy leg, he had an uncanny ability to appear out of nowhere.

'What do you mean, master?' asked Rake.

'Alida has gone missing,' said Salt. 'When I returned to the armoury workshop this evening, I found her absent and the task I assigned her unfinished. This struck me as out of character. She is the most reliable of all of you.'

The others didn't protest. Snow *was* completely dependable.

'When I sought her out, to request an explanation, I could not find her. I wondered if for some reason she had come here, to the Old School.' He frowned. 'I found her armour out of storage and her medallion and helmet missing.'

'I thought it was a bit odd when she didn't show up in the canteen at tea,' said Rake.

Oddball looked puzzled. 'Why would she want just her medallion and helmet?'

'What about her cadet ID belt?' asked Tea-Leaf. 'Had she taken that off?'

'Not to my knowledge,' replied Salt.

''Cos if she's still wearing that,' continued Tea-Leaf, 'she *must* be in the Academy somewhere. Otherwise the alarm would have gone off again.'

Hoax looked a bit shifty. 'Not necessarily. Last night, after Stamper got slimed and I blew my cover, they realized it was a false alarm – that there was no escapee. So they stopped searching for the ID belt. But they couldn't get the alarm to stop. In the end, they decided to shut down the system temporarily. I don't think it's back on yet.'

'It isn't,' confirmed Salt. 'Which means that Alida could have left the complex, even wearing her belt. If she has, we need to find her as soon as possible.'

'But why would Snow go off without telling anyone?' said Rake. 'Like you said, master, she's the reliable one. It's just not like her.'

Salt let out a long sigh. He scanned his trainees' concerned faces, uncertain how much to share with them.

'Alida has been experiencing some unsettling

mental disturbances,' he said slowly. 'I believe she may be in a somewhat troubled state of mind.'

The others exchanged knowing glances. Rake spoke for all of them.

'There's something different about her, isn't there, master?'

'She can make stuff move without touching it, for starters,' blurted Oddball. 'I'd swear she made that PShooter ball swerve last night—'

'And sometimes it's like she knows what's going on in someone else's head,' put in Tea-Leaf. 'She saw through that creep Ulcer way before the rest of us.'

Ulcer was a Byelon shape-shifter. The knights had recently had a near-fatal encounter with her.

Salt paused again. Then he nodded his heavy head slowly.

'I have reason to believe it likely that Alida will indeed prove to have . . . unusual abilities.'

'Freaky mind powers, more like,' Hoax murmured.

Salt chose to ignore him. 'But now is not the time to speculate on what those might be. Our priority is to find her and bring her home.' He addressed Oddball and Tea-Leaf directly. 'False-

Light, Balista – get suited up immediately. I have an assignment outside the Academy for the pair of you.'

'Why not me and Oddball?' complained Rake. As always, he was keen to be at the heart of the action.

'This particular mission requires your comrades' specialist skills in stealth and deception,' replied Salt.

'Why? What are we going to do?' asked Tea-Leaf eagerly. She could already sense the familiar mixture of nervousness and excitement rising inside her.

'If Alida is out in the city,' growled Salt, 'our only real chance of tracing her is to assume that she is still wearing her identity belt. The Corporation police scanners in SeeBlock can pinpoint any specified ID belt anywhere within the Limits. I want the pair of you to find a way inside SeeBlock and secretly access the scanner data.'

Hoax blew out his cheeks. 'Is that all?'

SeeBlock was the centre of police surveillance, from where the Chairman kept a close eye on each and every one of Nu-Topia's citizens. It was a high-security Corporation facility. The knights wouldn't just be able to stroll in and ask to borrow the tracking system.

Salt looked unapologetic. 'I have every faith that you and Balista can fulfil the mission. And we have little choice. Without using the Corporation scanners, we have no way to locate our friend.' He raised his bushy eyebrows. 'Unless you have a better suggestion, False-Light?'

Hoax shook his head meekly.

'So how do we get from here to SeeBlock?' asked Tea-Leaf.

Salt gave a wry smile. 'You have False-Light's . . . ingenuity to thank for my proposed solution to that problem. You will travel via refuse vehicle.'

'Huh?' Hoax frowned. 'The slops wagon?'

'Its nightly collection round takes it to most of the buildings in the city's central sector,' explained Salt. 'Even SeeBlock. If you can slip on board when it calls at the Academy, you should be able to hitch a ride to the police building undetected. Find the scanner consoles, obtain a fix on Alida's location, then make your way back here, as quickly as possible. And don't be seen.'

Ignoring Hoax's dismayed look, Salt turned to Rake and Oddball.

'In the meantime, you two will help me scour the Academy once more. It's still possible that Alida is somewhere in the compound – though I am all but convinced otherwise.'

He scanned their faces.

'Everyone clear?'

They nodded.

'And remember,' rumbled Salt, 'Stand Together . . .'

'Battle as One,' chorused his team.

For whatever reason, Snow had put herself in danger.

It was up to them to bring her in.

# Chapter 4
## Operation SeeBlock

'Remind me never to let the old man sort out our travel arrangements again,' hissed Hoax.

His body was jammed awkwardly inside a vertical metal chute about a metre across. Tea-Leaf was wedged in just above him, feet and hands braced against the chute's slimy walls.

The smell inside the chute was pretty revolting. But it was nothing compared to the stomach-turning stench they had had to endure inside the slops wagon itself. They had tried to block the reek by closing the nasal filters on their helmets, but it had still seeped through. When the vehicle had finally reached the main waste reservoir of the SeeBlock building and the two young knights had been able to scramble out of the wagon and up into one of the narrow chutes leading from the giant tank, the rank atmosphere had seemed almost pleasant by comparison.

'A *really* bad smell can eventually drive you loopy, you know?' said Hoax. 'My dad lost two good men that way when his special forces unit were fighting in the Ionian sulphur swamps.'

Tea-Leaf snorted.

'You just can't help yourself, can you?' she whispered. 'Your father never went anywhere near Io. He was a second-hand shuttle salesman. Rake told me.'

'Aaahhhh,' replied Hoax mysteriously. 'That was what he *wanted* people to believe . . .'

Tea-Leaf gave a weary sigh. She decided to change the subject.

'When is this clacking thing going to get us somewhere?' she said. 'Are you *sure* this one leads to the kitchens?'

They must have climbed fifty metres by now, inching their way awkwardly up the cramped chute. Tea-Leaf was making full use of her gauntlets' hi-grab fingertips, but was still finding the slimy metal surface hard to grip.

Hoax was having an even tougher time. He had twice slithered back an alarming distance before managing to wedge himself in place again.

Hoax slid the microfilm diagram of the police building's layout across his visor, studied it, then withdrew it again.

'Yup, this is the one. Unless the plans Salt gave us are wrong.'

Tea-Leaf grunted and continued to wriggle up the chute. After climbing a few more difficult metres in silence, she suddenly gave a more encouraging sound.

'Yes!'

'What is it?'

'Hatch, just above me. I reckon we're there.'

Light leaked into the murky shaft as Tea-Leaf cautiously swung the hatch-flap open. She was silent for a few seconds, then whispered down to Hoax below.

'Looks like the right place to me! And there's nobody about.'

Although it was the middle of the night, they both knew that SeeBlock would be far from deserted. The Chairman expected to be able to find out where anyone in Nu-Topia was, at any time of day or night. His surveillance teams worked round the clock. So the two young Armouron took care to make no noise as they eased themselves through the hatch into the kitchen area.

Tea-Leaf grabbed a hand towel from a rail beside one of the kitchen's several sinks.

'Clean up a bit – otherwise anyone who doesn't spot us will *smell* us coming!' she hissed. She began hurriedly wiping the grime from her grey armour.

'Watch and learn,' whispered Hoax. He pressed a micro-switch on his wrist. Each separate plate of his armour instantly shed a wafer-thin layer from its surface. The slivers of muck-smeared armour fell to the floor, leaving Hoax's orange suit gleaming once more.

'I know Salt designed it as an evasive feature,' beamed Hoax, 'but it does have *other* uses.' He gave Tea-Leaf a smug wink.

'Very clever,' hissed Tea-Leaf. As she finished cleaning herself up, Hoax gathered up his shed flakes of armour in another towel and shoved them through the waste hatch.

'Where now?' asked Tea-Leaf. Hoax checked his visor microfilm again.

'According to this, there are several areas on this floor that should have a tracking console. We need to find one not in use, so you can hack in.'

He moved to the doorway of the kitchen area and peered both ways along the grey-walled corridor that ran past it.

'All clear!' he hissed. 'If we go right, the second room on the left should have a tracking console.'

They moved swiftly and silently along the corridor. The colour of Tea-Leaf's armour seemed to lighten slightly, to blend in with the pale grey walls.

As they passed the first door, Tea-Leaf suddenly halted. She lifted her right hand to the side of her helmet. Hoax recognized the gesture. Her suit and medallion heightened all her senses. Her acute hearing had picked up something.

'We've got company!' she whispered urgently. 'Kettles, by the sounds of their footfalls! Three, maybe four, coming our way!'

The corridor turned sharply to the right about ten metres ahead – just beyond the door they were heading for. If a patrol of White Knights was about to come round the corner, they were hopelessly exposed.

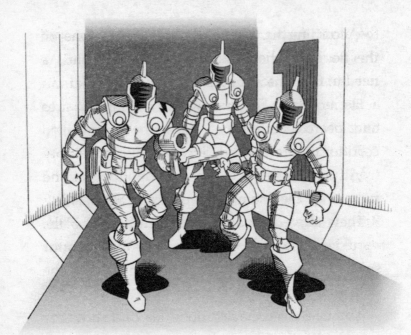

Instinctively, Hoax withdrew his staff and snapped it into nunchaku form, ready for the fight.

'No, you dunk-head!' hissed Tea-Leaf. 'Salt said in and out without being seen!' She hastily hit the door release on the wall beside her, dragged Hoax into the room on their left and sealed the door behind them.

It only took a moment for Tea-Leaf to realize she had made a mistake. The door had led them into the near end of the same room as

✺ ⚜ 🜂 ✪ 🕸 🅰 ☉-🜁 🜔 ◉ ⬡

the door further along the corridor – one of the tracker console rooms. At its far end, a female computer operator was sitting at an active terminal. Fortunately, she didn't appear to have heard them enter.

Both knights ducked down behind an empty workstation. As they did so, the door at the far end of the room slid open and three White Knights strode through it. The one with a black shoulder flash took a step forward. The operator spun round in her chair to greet it.

'Yes, Captain? How can I help?'

'I request a tracking scan to assist with a police manhunt,' said the White Knight flatly.

The woman nodded. She turned to face her computer display and spoke directly into it.

'Level nine access requested.'

There was a soft bleep, then the woman turned back to the White Knight.

'What are the individual's details?'

'Citizen number 23673911,' droned the android. 'A fugitive, guilty of power-usage violations.'

The operator tapped away at her keyboard for a few seconds before speaking again.

'I have a fix. You'll find your target in sector

NW47. He's in the roof space of the old hospital building.'

The White Knight captain turned abruptly and left the room, accompanied by its fellow androids. The door sliced shut behind them.

The woman returned to staring at her screen, her back to Hoax and Tea-Leaf. A moment or two later, she gave a loud yawn and stretched wearily.

Hoax tapped Tea-Leaf on the shoulder guard, nodded meaningfully at the operator, then mimed the action of drawing a bow.

Tea-Leaf nodded back. She silently slipped her crossbow from her back. Opening a compartment in its side, she took out a needle-tipped dart. She loaded the dart and took aim.

There was a *fsssh-thutt* sound and the woman slumped forward onto her keyboard, the tranquillizer dart sticking from her neck.

The two knights hurried forward to check on her. Tea-Leaf gently pulled out the dart.

'She'll be fine. There's only enough stuff in one of these to put her out for a few minutes. When she comes round, she'll just think she dropped off.'

She wheeled the operator's chair to one side and

took up her place in front of the console. Flipping open a compartment in her leg armour, she pulled out her trusty computer-hacking kit.

'Funny, really,' she said, as she unfurled the roll-up keyboard and attached its hack-patch to the back of the console. 'This is one place I can link up without worrying about being detected. Even the Corporation wouldn't scan for activity inside its own surveillance centre!'

'It's like the calm at the eye of the storm,' agreed Hoax.

Tea-Leaf grinned. She cracked her knuckles – making Hoax wince – then set to work. Her fingers skipped lightly across the keyboard like those of a talented musician playing an instrument. Her keen eyes focused intently on the streams of code now scrolling across the display.

'Right then. Let's see what we can dig up, shall we?'

But after a minute or so of non-stop tippety-tapping, her eager expression faded. She began to look increasingly vexed. She broke off abruptly, thumped the desktop and gave a snarl of frustration.

'Dunk!'

Hoax leaned in to look at the display screen.

'What's the problem?'

'I can't get past the security log-in,' complained Tea-Leaf. 'It's a dual-layer access block.'

'Which in ordinary language means?'

'You need to clear two combined checks to get in. There's a basic key-in password – I've cracked that, no problem. But to use the tracking system, you need to provide a biometric identity-check too – something specific to each individual operator authorized to use the system.'

'What? A thumb-print? A retina-scan?' quizzed Hoax.

'A digital voice signature,' said Tea-Leaf. 'I can't get in without an exact vocal match to this workstation's designated operator.' She nodded towards the slumped woman. 'Sleeping Beauty here. That's what she was doing a moment ago – logging in vocally. But she must have logged out after the scan.'

Hoax waved away Tea-Leaf's worries. He evidently didn't see the problem.

'Why didn't you say so sooner?' he said. 'I might not understand half your computer-speak gobbledegook, but voice impressions I *can* do.'

Of course. Tea-Leaf could have kicked herself. Salt had designed the helmet of Hoax's suit specifically to enhance his natural talent for mimicry. His medallion too boosted his impressionist skills. It was worth a try, at least.

Hoax leaned a little closer to the tiny microphone built into the computer display's surround and began to speak.

Except it wasn't *him* speaking.

It was uncanny. Modified by his helmet's unique acoustics, the pitch, tone and modulation of his voice were exactly like those of the SeeBlock operator. It was as if he had stolen the woman's voice.

'Level nine access requested,' he purred.

A moment later, there was a cheery *blee-blip* and the display filled with the main scanner menu.

Tea-Leaf returned her friend's broad grin.

'We're in!'

She swiftly disconnected her hacking equipment and began tapping away on the computer's own keyboard.

'Have you still got Snow's ID belt code?'

Hoax rooted about for the slip of paper that Salt had given him. As he quickly read off the chain of letters and numbers, Tea-Leaf keyed them in.

Less than a minute after clearing the security log-in, they had what they had come for – an exact fix on Snow's whereabouts.

The two friends looked at one another, then back at the screen to double-check. Hoax raised his eyebrows.

'Well. That's unexpected. Wonder what old Salt'll make of *that*.'

'She's *where*?!' Salt looked at Tea-Leaf in pure disbelief.

'Bay Three of the Nu-Topia spaceport freight terminal,' repeated Tea-Leaf.

'Or at least,' added Oddball, 'that's where the SeeBlock scanners last got a fix on her ID belt. It didn't show up at all on the most recent scans, which is a bit weird.'

The two young knights were now safely back in the Old School. Their return trip from SeeBlock had gone very smoothly. Once Tea-Leaf had located the relevant data on the Corporation tracking system, they had made a swift and silent exit from the console room – not a moment too soon, as the doped operator was showing signs of reviving.

A wild rubbish-chute ride from the kitchen had dumped them unceremoniously back in the building's main waste reservoir. They had escaped the tank via one of its pressure-release outlets, then clambered down its maintenance gantry to reach ground level. After slipping away from the back of the SeeBlock Tower and attempting to clean themselves up a little, they had begun making their way back to the Academy across the darkened city.

The last stage of their journey – reaching the secret passage in the Academy garage – had been fairly straightforward, now the Corporation shuttle had gone. Without its android guards on the prowl, it had been simple enough to slip through the hidden wall door and rejoin Salt, Rake and Oddball.

They had found their friends eager for news. Their own thorough search of the Academy had turned up no trace of Snow. But Tea-Leaf and Oddball's report had put puzzled looks, not smiles, on their faces.

'What's she doing at the spaceport?' wondered Oddball out loud.

'I have no idea,' growled Salt. He fell silent for a few seconds, lost in thought. Then he spoke to Tea-Leaf again. 'Bay Three, you said? Is there any way of tracing recent activity in that bay? It may give us some clue to why Alida found herself there.'

'I'm way ahead of you, master!' said Tea-Leaf proudly. 'Once we got the fix on her location, I used the SeeBlock spyware to have a quick snoop around the spaceport's flight-scheduling server. Honestly, getting past their firewall was clacking child's play . . .'

'And?' pressed Salt impatiently.

Tea-Leaf got back to the point. 'There were only two ships scheduled to depart from Bay Three today,' she reported. 'One of them left early this morning – before Snow went missing. Maybe Snow was interested in the other one for some reason – the one that left this evening. I copied its destination from the flight schedule.'

She handed the scrap of paper with Snow's ID code on one side to Salt. She had scribbled a name on its reverse.

'I wrote it down in case I didn't remember it right,' said Tea-Leaf. 'I've never heard of it before.

Does it ring any bells with you, master?'

But Salt didn't seem to hear her. He was staring at the piece of paper in his hand. Much of the colour had drained from his aged face. Finally, without looking up, he spoke.

'Templer. Sappar.' His voice was a low, grim growl. 'Put on your armour. Immediately.'

'What is it, master?' pressed Rake.

Salt lifted his gaze at last. His typically calm eyes blazed with fierce determination.

'We're going after her.'

# Chapter 5
## The Creature

Snow's world was shaking. As consciousness seeped back into her mind, she was vaguely aware of something squeezing her shoulders tightly.

Hands.

But it wasn't Salt's firm, reassuring grip this time. These fingers had the hard, cold feel of metal.

Snow opened her eyes – to stare straight into the visored face of a White Knight.

Satisfied that it had roused her, the android guard stopped shaking her roughly.

'Your presence in this sector is unauthorized,' it droned. 'Identify yourself.'

The adrenalin rush of panic brought information

flooding back into Snow's mind. She was in the cargo pod, in the garage. She'd been checking out the yellow canister when she'd fallen. This guard must have found her.

'I repeat, remove your headgear and state your citizen identity code immediately,' commanded the White Knight.

Headgear. Snow felt a rush of relief. Of course – she still had her helmet on! Which meant that she hadn't exposed her real identity. Yet.

Without further hesitation, Snow went into action.

The White Knight was stooping over her, having hauled her into a sitting position. Its hands were still gripping her shoulders.

Snow brought her own arms up between the android's, swinging them up and out. Her self-defence move broke the robot's grip. Rocking backwards, she tucked up her legs, then thrust a fierce double-footed kick into the White Knight's chest. It toppled backwards, clattering against the wall of the cargo pod.

Snow was on her feet in an instant. She dived through the gap between the pod's partly opened sides, out into the garage.

Except that it wasn't the garage.

Snow's sore head spun. Instead of the familiar scene she had expected, she appeared to be in the middle of a large, open hangar. There were numerous people in white uniforms bustling about the area. To her left loomed the vast hulk of a freight-carrying starship, from which cargo pods were being unloaded by a squad of White Knights.

Her brain struggled to process what she was seeing.

*They must have loaded the pod with me still inside!* she realized. While she'd been unconscious, the pod had presumably left the Academy in the Corporation shuttle she'd seen, then been loaded on the freight ship beside her.

*So where on Earth am I now?*

She caught sight of a large transparent section in one of the hangar's walls and realized, with gut-churning shock, that she wasn't anywhere on Earth. The strange landscape visible through the window was clearly not terrestrial.

Snow knew that the Corporation had outposts throughout the galaxy. This must be one of them. Judging by the scientific-looking staff milling about, she guessed it was some sort of research station.

'Halt! You are under arrest!'

Snow's confusion had cost her valuable seconds. The White Knight she had knocked down came staggering out of the pod behind her. The sound of its yell drew the attention of its fellow androids and several of the human staff.

Snow ran. She made it to the passageway leading from the hangar before the Corporation guards could give chase.

She sprinted along the passage, then darted down another, hoping to shake off her pursuers. This short corridor had no side-branches. It brought Snow to a transparent door, through which she could see the rocky, bluish-grey terrain outside. But she couldn't get the door to open.

Snow could hear the pursuing party approaching fast. Without her Armouron suit and tonfa – her T-shaped combat baton – a fight would be futile. She looked around desperately for somewhere to hide.

A few metres back along the corridor, there was a domed skylight in the ceiling. Snow dashed back to stand beneath it. She squatted, then leaped up to grab the thin ledge around its rim. Clinging on with her fingertips, she hauled herself up, then wedged her body inside the clear dome.

Only seconds later, the White Knights burst into the corridor. Snow watched them charge past beneath her. She pressed herself up tight against the skylight.

She saw the guards come to a halt at the transparent door, realizing with a sinking feeling that if she could see them, they would be able to see her when they turned. For the moment, though, they had their backs to her.

'This is the definitely the route the fugitive took,' asserted the guard with the black shoulder flash – the unit's captain. 'She must have activated the emergency exit door. Search outside.'

One of the other androids took a slim keycard from its belt. It swiped it across a domed sensor and the door slid open.

Snow's hand slipped a fraction against the skylight's smooth surface, making a very slight squeak. The White Knight bringing up the rear turned its head.

In a flash, Snow dropped to the floor and dashed past the huddle of guards, out through the open doorway. A moment later, they were after her, like hounds running down a fox.

Snow sprinted desperately away from the research station. She made it ten metres across the rocky ground, then twenty, then thirty. She had no idea where she was running to – only that she must keep going, must not be caught. Thirty-five metres . . . forty . . .

Then, suddenly, all thoughts of escape were driven from Snow's mind by an explosion of raw pain that seemed to detonate in her brain. It wasn't the cry of a voice this time – just a paralysing flare of white-hot agony.

As Snow staggered forward and fell, the pain suddenly diminished, as though she had stumbled past its point of greatest intensity.

Her mind still thumping with shockwaves of pain, Snow struggled onto her hands and knees and scrabbled desperately forward across the dusty terrain, expecting to feel the metal grip of a White Knight at any moment. After dragging herself as far as she could from the invisible barrier, she slumped down once more, unable to continue. With difficulty, she rolled over, craned her neck and looked back.

The scene that met her eyes was like nothing she had ever witnessed before. The White Knights who had been pursuing her were not far from where she had fallen. But for the moment they were paying her no attention. Instead, they were engaged in a violent battle with – *what*?

Snow shook her throbbing head, then stared again at the bizarre, alien creature. It was hovering in the air above the Knights, beating huge wings that fanned out behind its long, jointed forelimbs. As she watched, it reared up to slash at the androids with the curved claws of its hind feet.

It was enormous – at least five metres from wing-tip to wing-tip. The only flying creatures Snow could think of that compared in size were the legendary prehistoric beasts she had read about in the Academy library's data-files. Pterosaurs, that was it. This strange creature's featherless, leathery wings, anchored to its arms and sides, reminded her of those ancient monsters.

But the creature's resemblance to any beast Snow knew of ended there. It had a peculiar elongated head, which was fringed along each side with a thin, rigid, brightly coloured frill. Its long brow was topped by a bony crest. Its short,

thick neck was rooted in bulging shoulders that powered its massive wings. Behind them, its body tapered towards its slim tail-end. Other than the grey membranes of its wings, its outlandish body was covered with thick interlocking plates of some coarse, stony material.

As the creature wheeled round to attack the group of White Knights from another angle, Snow noticed something particularly odd. Below its narrow eyes, there was no sign of a nose or mouth. And despite the ferocity of its attack, the beast was making no sound whatsoever. It seemed natural that it should roar or screech as it set upon the White Knights. But it was fighting them in complete silence.

Its assault was so savage that two of the Corporation androids had gone down already and the remainder were in retreat. The creature drove them backwards, until they reached the point where Snow had painfully burst through the invisible wall.

As the White Knights continued to fall back, the flying creature swooped after them – and its vast body suddenly went rigid. It began to spasm, as though suffering some kind of fit. It veered violently aside and crumpled to the ground, in obvious agony.

*Like it hit something*, thought Snow's aching brain. *Just like I did. As if there's some sort of barrier it can't pass . . .*

The White Knights seized their chance to advance on the stricken creature. But it was quicker than Snow to recover. It struggled into an upright position, standing on its wing-tips, like a primate resting on its knuckles. By the time the first android lunged at it, it was ready. The

White Knight went down, wires spilling from its electronic innards, its armour torn open by a razor-sharp wing-tip.

Three down!

The other guards retreated warily once more – but only to just beyond the invisible barrier. They seemed well aware that the creature could not get through it from the outside.

The unit's captain peered across to where Snow lay. She sensed that it was analysing the pros and cons of trying to capture her while the alien beast was still on the rampage out there.

It clearly decided against it, for a moment later it gave a swift hand-signal and the remaining White Knights turned and trudged back towards the research station.

The creature watched the retreating androids until they re-entered the compound. Then it turned slowly, lurching from one wing-tip to the other in its peculiar fashion and fixed its yellow eyes on Snow.

## Chapter 6
### Field Trip

Nu-Topia's new spaceport was one of the city's most impressive landmarks.

Viewed from above, the giant, round building looked rather like a huge cog, or the wheel of an ancient ship. Each of the short spurs sticking out around its edge led to a separate landing platform. The majority of these platforms were used for terrestrial shuttles – craft carrying people or freight to and fro from Earth's other major cities. A dozen were reserved for interplanetary vehicles – starships that were coming from, or going out to, some distant galactic settlement.

The spaceport's circular structure housed passenger and cargo terminals, shops, a holovidtheatre and much more. It squatted on a wide pedestal base, which raised it about thirty metres from the ground. Transparent elevators climbed the base's silvered sides, carrying citizens from street level to the bustling terminal complex above.

The Perfect Corporation had built the port several years ago. It was heralded as a triumph of up-to-the-minute technology and cutting-edge design. The Chairman himself had promoted it as a flagship project – a shining example of the Corporation's commitment to building a Perfect World.

In reality, the Chairman had built the spaceport only to increase his control over the lives of Nu-Topia's citizens. Once it was completed, he quickly saw to it that it became the only way in and out of the city for major transport. Smaller docking stations scattered here and there were demolished. The hidden surveillance systems built into the impressive new terminal gave the Corporation a complete picture of who and what was moving in and out of the city. The people strolling happily around the gleaming new passenger lounges were blissfully unaware that they were under such close scrutiny.

Most of them were equally unaware of what was going on under their feet. The spaceport's base did far more than simply support its upper structure. It was inside this lower part of the building, which few people ever entered, that some of the most impressive technology of all was in action.

The Basement, as it was known by the spaceport staff, was where the complicated business of sorting and loading the endless stream of cargo that flowed through the city's port took place.

The whole system was automated. A complex network of interconnecting mag-lev rails filled the entire Basement, leading to and from each of the port's many dispatch and delivery points. Day and night, cargo pods of all shapes and sizes moved smoothly along the trackway, floating on its invisible magnetic field.

Right now, there was something else moving around the dimly lit Basement too. Four shadowy forms were slinking between the mag-lev rails, ducking from one ceiling-support pillar to the next – a broad-set old man in a rough tunic, accompanied by three smaller figures in brightly coloured armour . . .

Rake halted beside one of the pillars and read the large laser-etched number on its side.

'Fifty-eight,' he whispered, as his companions stole across to join him. 'This is it. This is where Tea-Leaf said to meet her.'

Without Tea-Leaf to guide them, the group would have struggled to find their way safely to the spaceport in the first place. Their streetwise friend's experience of navigating the city by night had really paid off – again.

Having led them into the Basement via a loose vent cover, Tea-Leaf had now slunk off to try and find out more about any recent activity in Bay Three. She had promised to rejoin them at the specified pillar.

Just beyond it, one of the mag-lev tracks branched to form a siding. A line of three cargo pods floated motionless on this dead-end section of track. The young knights and their mentor settled down behind them to wait for their friend.

'Just *how* clacking cool is this system, eh, guys?' said Oddball.

He was gazing in delight at the cargo pods gliding silently along their tracks. As he watched another pod pass, he pointed at a small convex disc clamped to its side.

'Every pod has a tag that tells the system which loading bay it's meant to end up at,' he enthused. 'Then there's a tag-scanner before each track junction, so that the pod is switched onto the right route. Simple, but brilliant!'

Hoax gave him a despairing look. 'You need help, mate,' he said. 'Nobody should be *that* into technology. You're like some sort of ultra-geek.'

Rake wasn't really listening to either of them. He was looking around anxiously. He was getting impatient with all this skulking about. He wanted to do something.

'I wonder what's taking her so long,' he said anxiously. 'It's a bit of a maze down here – maybe she's got lost.'

'Lost?' said a familiar voice behind and above him. Tea-Leaf dropped lightly to the floor a few metres away, then strode over to join them. 'I don't think so! I've spent too much time down here not to know my way around!'

Rake gave her an intrigued look. 'How come? Why hang out here?'

'The first time I found my way in, I was just looking for somewhere dry to sleep,' said Tea-Leaf. 'But I ran into a gang of tough-nuts from East Two. They'd come in here now and then, break a cargo pod open, then do a runner with whatever was inside.' She sounded a little uncomfortable. 'We struck a deal.' She nodded towards the far side of the Basement, lost in darkness. 'The pods are all security scanned back there, to check out their contents. I used to hack into the scanner output, so I could tell the East Two boys which pods had stuff worth stealing in. In return, they'd give me a cut.'

She noticed Salt's disapproving expression.

'It's no picnic out here, you know,' she said defensively. 'I had to eat.'

'Anyway,' said Oddball, 'what did you find out about Snow?'

Tea-Leaf was happy to change the subject.

'There *was* a ship that left Bay Three at twenty-one hundred,' she began. 'That's just after the SeeBlock scan placed her there. It was a Corporation freighter, heading direct to Kasteesh.'

Kasteesh. The destination she had written down for Salt. The name that had caused him to react with such uncharacteristic alarm.

'It looks like Snow was on that flight then,' said Oddball. 'If she wasn't, her ID belt would have shown up since. The SeeBlock systems are set up to track anywhere inside the Limits. Snow taking a trip out of Nu-Topian airspace would explain why she'd dropped off the recent scans.'

Salt gave a heavy sigh. 'Then we must assume that she is indeed on her way to Kasteesh,' he rumbled. 'And we must find a way to follow.' He paused to think. 'The chances of our finding another transport heading directly to such an isolated planet are slight. I fear our only hope is to seek a trade ship whose pilot we can bribe to divert course. That won't be easy.'

'But, master,' said Rake, frowning, 'how can we go after her at all? Won't we be missed back at the Academy?'

'Not immediately, Templer,' replied the old armourer. 'I anticipated that our recovery of Alida could be . . . complicated. So I took advantage of a friendship to set up a cover story for our absence.'

Hoax gave a cheeky smirk. 'Did you now, you wily old devil?'

Salt remained grave. 'I have an old comrade, Rajsim, who manages a smelting compound south of the city. Not one of our order, but sympathetic to our cause. As far as Brand and the other Academy supervisors are concerned, I have taken you, Templer, False-Light and Sappar, as well as young Alida, to a four-day training course at the smelting plant. If questioned, Rajsim will know to confirm this story.'

'We're on a field trip!' grinned Hoax. 'Excellent!'

Rake nodded his head, impressed.

'OK, so we have a little time, at least – just no way of going after her.'

'Whoa there!' said Tea-Leaf. 'I know it's against the odds, but there is another ship setting off for Kasteesh. It came up on the scheduling system when I was checking up on the Bay Three stuff. It's loading right now – departs from Bay Nine within the hour, in fact. And you'll never guess whose ship it is . . .'

The others looked at her expectantly.

'Only the Chairman's!' she hissed.

'The executive shuttle?' growled Salt. 'Are you sure?'

Tea-Leaf nodded confidently.

Salt's face darkened. 'Why would the Chairman be going there? Why now?' he murmured. 'Still' – his eyes flashed with purpose – 'if his is the only ship bound for Kasteesh, we must find a way to be on it when it departs!'

'But how the clack do we do that?' said Hoax. 'It's not like we can just stroll up and say "Excuse me, Chairman, can we have a lift?" His shuttle will have more Kettles crawling over it than any other ship in port!'

'And you don't even have your armour, master,' added Rake. 'If anyone catches sight of you with us, it's game over.'

Salt's Armouron suit was currently unfit for use. It had been badly mangled during the group's recent memorable encounter with the Armournaut.

There was a long silence, as five brains desperately sought a solution to their predicament. Suddenly, Oddball gave a 'Yes!', sprang to his feet and turned to stare eagerly at the line of cargo pods behind them.

'Of course!'

The others looked at him expectantly.

'Look! These three pods must have been shunted onto this siding-track because their tags tell the system that they're not needed yet, right?' he gabbled. 'They're being held here until whatever ship is meant to carry them is ready to load.'

He moved to the pod at the head of the line, flapped open a panel in his shoulder-guard and withdrew a flat-bladed screwdriver. Clutching the limpet-like tag device on the pod's side with one hand, he used the other to prise it off with the screwdriver.

He held out the tag to show the others.

'With a bit of luck, I should be able to tweak this thing's setting so that it tells the track scanners that this pod is meant to be loaded on the craft waiting in Bay Nine. That should mean it'll get pulled back online for immediate loading.'

Hoax was looking puzzled.

'How does getting this pod loaded on the Chairman's ship help us?'

But Rake's face suddenly lit up.

'Because we're going to be hiding inside it! Right, Oddball?'

'Exactly!' beamed Oddball. 'And we should be safe from detection,' he rambled on, 'because, like Tea-Leaf said just now, the pod's contents will already have been security scanned back there.'

He twisted off the cover of the tag device, then converted his screwdriver into a tweezer-like tool and began poking around inside it.

'I'll get this set up. It might take a little while. You lot see if you can get the pod open and cleared out a bit, so that there's room for us inside.'

Tea-Leaf looked at the cargo pod doubtfully.

'The magna-seals on these things are really strong,' she said. 'To stand any chance of breaking them open, we'll need something pretty rock solid and to hit them pretty hard.'

There was a series of quiet *crunch-click* sounds, rather like someone cracking their knuckles. Rake raised his right hand. His armoured gauntlet was scrunched in a formidable fist. Its tough plastallic parts had locked together to give it complete rigidity. He gave Tea-Leaf a broad grin.

'You called, madam?'

# Chapter 7
## The Shattered City

Snow's mind had more or less recovered from the effects of her collision with the invisible barrier. But now she had a different reason to feel dizzy. She was dangling precariously fifty metres above the rocky landscape below her, clutched in the massive claws of the flying alien creature.

When the beast had first snatched her up, as she tried desperately to crawl away, she had been surprised that it had grasped her so carefully. From its appearance and the ferocity of its attack on the White Knights, she had fully expected it to slice her into ribbons there and then. Instead, as it loomed over her, it had taken hold of her almost gently. Then, with a series of powerful wing-beats, it had launched itself into the air, carrying her high into the sky.

By now, they had flown quite some distance from the research compound. Once Snow had got over her initial brain-numbing panic, she had tried to take in some of the awesome view. The terrain that stretched out below her was rocky, lifeless and hostile. The further the creature flew, the more mountainous the landscape became.

*What is this place?* thought Snow. *And how in the world did I get here?*

Since coming round from being unconscious, she hadn't had time to try and figure out what had happened to her. The last familiar thing she remembered was the Academy garage. Everything since – the chase, the invisible wall, this bizarre creature – made no sense to her.

The giant beast suddenly banked steeply to the right. They swooped low over the crest of a ridge that joined the summits of a range of tall, steep-sided peaks. What lay beyond the ridge took Snow's breath away.

A vast city covered the opposite face of the mountain. But it was a city unlike any on Earth. Instead of buildings of concrete, glass and metal, it was constructed from stone, the natural material of the mountainside. The rocky terrain had been carved and shaped into hundreds of giant spheres. There was a circular opening in the upper face of each. Snow could see as they flew over them that the spheres were hollow inside. They reminded her of the galls created by insects from the bark of trees. But here, the galls were of rock and truly massive.

The creature began a spiralling descent. As it flew lower, Snow noticed that much of the strange city was in a state of dereliction. Many of the hollow rock spheres were badly fractured, or partly collapsed. Whole clusters had been reduced to crumbling ruins by some destructive force. Only the very central area, comprising half a dozen of the biggest spheres, appeared undamaged.

Snow's heart missed a beat as the creature suddenly plummeted towards the roof-opening of the largest of this cluster. Moments later, she found herself circling its interior – a cavernous rock-walled chamber.

The winged alien flew towards a narrow ledge that jutted out from the cavern's concave wall. It deposited Snow carefully on this ledge, then swooped away, to alight on a high stone pillar that rose from the cavern's floor.

Snow got to her feet, still giddy from her stomach-churning flight. Her mind turned instantly to escape. But it was clear why the creature had dropped her where it had. There was no way off the ledge. It was a long drop to the floor below and there was a wall of solid rock behind her.

The creature was watching her from its rock perch – one of several columns grouped in a horseshoe shape around the cavern. Snow was alarmed to see several more creatures, much the same as the first in appearance, settled on the other columns.

The stone columns and parts of the cavern walls, Snow noticed, were heavily engraved with elaborate carvings – strange geometric patterns, whorls and motifs.

A low, booming voice suddenly echoed inside Snow's head.

*Why have you brought one of the Wingless to our council hall, Ko'Drall? They are our enemies, as you well know!*

Snow shook her head to clear it. She was sick of hearing voices. Somehow, though, she could sense that this one belonged to one of the bizarre alien gathering before her.

*Not all the Wingless have been our foes, my brother.*

This second voice was calmer, less hostile.

*This creature is an enemy of the Void Ones, it* continued. *I witnessed several of the metal monsters chasing her. An enemy of theirs may perhaps be a friend of ours. And look at the fashion of her head covering. It reminds me strongly of the device worn by the last Wingless One who was welcome among us.*

Snow was finding it utterly bizarre listening to a conversation in her head, while the creatures sat silently in front of her. It was pretty clear that the voice defending her belonged to the creature who had carried her here. She wondered which one of the others was the owner of the more suspicious voice.

As her eyes moved from one giant beast to the next, her heart suddenly jumped. Among the stone carvings on one of the columns, she noticed a familiar pattern. There it was again, on the wall! In fact, as her eyes eagerly scanned the cavern, she could make out the recognizable peak-shaped motif engraved in any number of places.

*The Armouron insignia!* cried her bewildered mind. *Why is the order's symbol carved on their walls?!*

As one, the creatures turned their yellow eyes on Snow. Despite the inhuman nature of their faces, their searching stares were clearly ones of intrigued astonishment. Snow sensed instinctively that they had overheard her last thoughts.

The creature she believed to be Ko'Drall suddenly leaped from its plinth and swooped towards her, alighting on the brink of her ledge. Snow took an involuntary step backwards and bumped into the rock wall immediately behind her.

As the creature's eyes met hers, a voice filled her head. It was far stronger and louder than before. Snow had no doubt that, for the first time, Ko'Drall was 'speaking' directly to her.

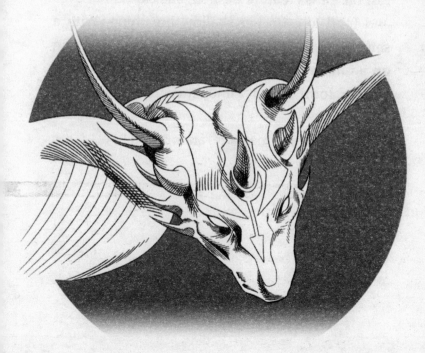

*Can you hear us, stranger?*

Snow pressed herself against the rock, uncertain how to react. Were they angry that she had been eavesdropping? The creature leaned closer, so that its peculiar mouthless face was only a metre from hers.

*If you can hear my thoughts, Wingless One, then answer them!*

Pulse pounding, Snow looked into the creature's deep, searching gaze. She nodded her head.

Then, sensing that this was not the method of response the creature desired, she closed her eyes and tried to calm her shallow breathing. With a sensation she had never felt before and drawing on an instinct she didn't understand, she let her answer form in her mind, then released it, like a bird.

*Yes*, her mind-message announced. *Yes. I can hear you.*

## Chapter 8
### The Riders of Kasteesh

'I just hope you rigged that tag-gadget right, Oddball,' said Hoax. 'You can't tell *what* ship we got ourselves loaded on from inside here. We could be heading for the wrong side of the galaxy, for all we know.'

He, Rake, Oddball, Tea-Leaf and Salt were huddled together inside the cargo pod, most of which was still crammed with its original contents – stacked crates of canned soya meat. It wasn't overly comfortable. At Salt's request, Oddball had crushed a couple of glo-caps, to provide a little light. Unlike the youngsters, the old armourer had no night-vision visor to rely on.

'Don't you worry,' smiled Oddball. 'I'm certain

we're heading to Kasteesh right now. Well – *almost* certain.'

'Fantastic,' said Hoax sarcastically. He plucked a can from the stack beside him. 'Oh well, at least we won't starve . . .'

Rake turned to Salt, who was hunched bear-like in silence.

'Master, we're going to be stuck inside here for quite a while. Why don't you explain what's so significant about Kasteesh, while we've got time on our hands. We all saw how you reacted when you found out that's where Snow was heading.'

Salt gave a grunt and shuffled awkwardly.

'Rake's right, master,' pressed Tea-Leaf. 'Why were you so shocked?'

Salt let out a sigh of resignation. 'We do have something of a trip ahead of us, I suppose,' he growled. 'And I see no real reason for further secrecy.'

There was a moment's silence, then he continued.

'Very well, Templer, Balista, Sappar and False-Light – I will tell you the story of Kasteesh. And of why, I fear, it has drawn our young friend into danger.'

The glo-caps' weak yellow gleam cast an eerie light over the faces of Salt's four young listeners as he began his tale.

'The connection between the Armouron and the planet of Kasteesh goes back many years,' rumbled the old armourer. 'Their destinies first became entangled a very long time ago.'

'What, when you were young?' blurted Rake. He realized a moment too late how that sounded. Salt gave him a hard stare.

'Even further back than that, Templer – if your imagination can grasp such a time-scale,' he growled dryly. 'Over five centuries ago, in fact. Back in the early days of star travel, before the Corporation Wars. When the Armouron were still the dominant force for order across the galaxy.

'One of the foremost Armouron at that time was a knight named Ocell.'

It was Hoax who interrupted this time.

'I knew an Ocell once. He played pro-league speedball with my dad. I remember when they won the . . .'

His voice trailed off, as he sensed the four withering stares aimed his way.

Salt tried again.

'Ocell was a great warrior, but something of a loner. He was happiest when undertaking solo missions for the order, however arduous or perilous. As starship technology developed, he took on the lonely role of exploring the galactic fringe – the outreaches of known space. One such voyage took him to the small, rocky fringe-world of Kasteesh.

'In those days, entering a planet's atmosphere was still a risky business. Ocell's ship crash-landed and he was badly injured. He would have died – but for a tremendous stroke of good fortune. Not only was Kasteesh a world where the atmosphere was fine for him to breathe, but it also proved to be one of the handful of fringe worlds that was populated. Ocell's wrecked ship was discovered by one of the planet's natives. His body was recovered and over the coming months he was nursed back to full health.'

'You're right – he *was* lucky,' said Oddball. 'Not all people would be so caring.'

'Not *people*, Sappar,' said Salt. 'The natives of Kasteesh, as Ocell was the first to discover, are a race of large winged creatures. We know a lot more about them now than was known then – there has been a Corporation research station on Kasteesh for over a decade. One of its scientists – a man from the Hotlands – was the first to give the creatures a name: the *mashetani-anga*, from the Afrik for "sky-demons". Most people call them the "Mshanga".

'But for Ocell, they were a nameless unknown, unlike any beings he had previously encountered. Even their means of communicating was alien.'

'A different language, you mean?' said Rake.

Salt shook his head. 'No. The Mshanga have no use for language. They have no vocal apparatus whatsoever. Instead, they speak to one another by transferring mind-waves. They're telepaths.'

'So how did they communicate with Ocell?' asked Tea-Leaf.

'With difficulty, at first. But this is the most astonishing part of his tale: with time and the creatures' help, Ocell developed the ability to transmit and receive basic mind-messages himself. He was far from being a full telepath, but he forged the beginnings of a link with their thought-based community.'

'Wicked!' said Hoax. 'Imagine being able to get inside each other's heads. How cool would that be?'

'You'd hate it,' said Tea-Leaf. 'Whenever you claimed to have royal blood, or a pet prawlkon, or some other load of dunk, everyone would see right through you.'

Hoax grinned.

'You said "with time", master,' said Rake. 'So did Ocell stay on Kasteesh for quite a while?'

'He never left,' replied Salt. 'The company of the Mshanga suited him better than the bustle and noise of life among humans. After living in their colony for many years, he was granted the ultimate token of acceptance. The creature which had first rescued him and done most to care for him allowed him to ride it in flight.'

Tea-Leaf looked at Salt a little awkwardly. 'This is all fascinating stuff, master – but what has it got to do with Snow? You said there was a connection between her and Kasteesh. So far, I don't see it.'

'Be patient, Balista,' growled Salt. 'All will become clear.' He cleared his throat, then frowned. 'Where was I?'

'Ocell riding one of the flying aliens,' said Oddball.

'Ah, yes. Ocell had little sense of it at the

✵ ♈ ⏛ ◉ ▩ Ⓐ ⬟ ⊘ ✺

time, but in riding one of the Mshanga, he was becoming the first of a select group of Armouron Knights who would do so. By the time of his death, the creatures' relationship with Ocell had broadened into a wider one with the order as a whole. The knight selected to be his successor and bear his medallion chose like him to live among the Kasteesh colony. He too was granted the right to ride one of the creatures.

'And so it continued. One knight from each generation of Armouron had the honour of becoming a Rider, paired to a mind-mate among the Mshanga. And with time, the creatures began to assist the order with their work enforcing peace and justice. It was a powerful union. The Riders and their flying mounts became one of the most feared and respected forces within the outer reaches of the galaxy.'

Salt paused and looked meaningfully at Tea-Leaf.

'And, now, Balista, we come to your question. What has all this to do with our young friend Snow? Well, if I tell you that she is unique among you in having a father who himself belonged to our order, can you perhaps hazard a guess?'

'Snow's dad was an Armouron?' said a bewildered Oddball.

Salt nodded.

'You mean . . . he wasn't one of these Riders you've been talking about, was he?' ventured Tea-Leaf.

Another slow nod from Salt.

'The last Rider, to be precise,' said the old man gravely. 'As you know, the Corporation has made it its business to bring down the Armouron. And since the Chairman established his scientific base on Kasteesh, the Mshanga colony has also come under threat. The ancient union between our order and the Mshanga has collapsed.'

'But Snow doesn't know any of this, does she?' said Rake. 'She thinks her mum and dad were Nu-Topians. She told me they both died in a blue flu outbreak!'

Salt looked suddenly very weary. 'I made a promise not to tell the child of her true ancestry when she first came into my care,' he said. 'Now it seems that somehow – somehow I don't understand – she has discovered it for herself. I cannot see why she should otherwise choose to journey to Kasteesh.'

'Well, she'll be able to tell us exactly what she's up to when we catch up with her, won't she?' said Rake, putting on an air of cheery determination. 'She can't be *that* far ahead of us. I reckon we should just be grateful that the executive shuttle happened to be heading out this way.'

Salt gave Rake a rare smile. 'I applaud your positive outlook, Templer,' he said. But his expression quickly became more grave. 'In truth, though, the Chairman's presence gives me additional cause for concern. I'd like to know why he too feels the need to visit Kasteesh at this particular moment in time. In my experience, having that weasel around is only ever a bad thing.'

His heavy brows knitted in a scowl.

'A *very* bad thing.'

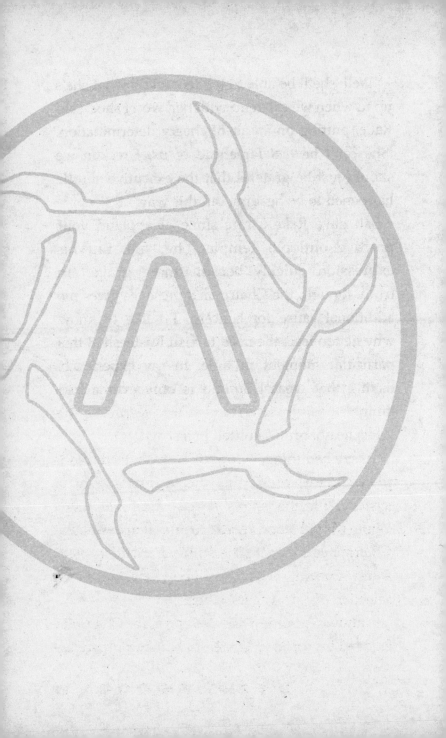

## Chapter 9
### A Welcome Break

The Chairman sat back in his lounger chair, took a sip from the glass of multi-coloured cocktail he held in one chubby hand, and admired the view of the receding Earth through the viewport of his executive shuttle's cabin.

Around him, his crew of human technicians were busily preparing the shuttle's control systems for the ship's spatial jump. A single White Knight stood rigidly to attention beside the Chairman's lounger. The android attendant held a tray carrying a jug of rainbow cocktail and a selection of extravagant nibbles.

Although he didn't like to admit it, the Chairman enjoyed his visits to Kasteesh. Not because of the planet itself, of course – that was mind-numbingly dreary. But spending time at the base there, which was manned only by Perfect Corp staff, gave the Chairman a chance to drop the tiresome pretence of being Mr Nice Guy. The absence of civilians meant he could relax and be himself for a while. He was free to bully and persecute at his whim – something he greatly enjoyed.

Not that this was a pleasure trip. The Chairman had important business to conduct. The alien prisoner that he had recently had transported to Earth from Kasteesh was being taken back to its home planet, on board a separate freight ship. The Chairman had important plans for the creature's fate – plans he wished to oversee himself.

Bringing the creature to Earth had proved to be a mistake. The Chairman had hoped that it would be a crowd-pulling attraction, fighting his Academy Gladiators. But the wretched beast had fallen ill. It had never made it into the Arena.

So now it was back to Plan A – trying to find a way to duplicate the alien creature's remarkable mental powers. As soon as he reached Kasteesh, he would see to it that the programme of research on the beast's brain-function was immediately restarted.

The experiments had been running since the creature's capture – for over a decade now – but without a major breakthrough. Perhaps the Corporation scientists would have more success with the Chairman breathing down their neck.

He was certain that his ultimate aim – to gain the use of mind-powers himself – was achievable. He had witnessed the psychic abilities of the human Armouron who had originally ridden the Kasteesh beast.

The Armouron. They were another reason that the Chairman wasn't sorry to leave Nu-Topia behind for a few days. In recent months, there had been worrying signs that his old adversaries had somehow become active in the city again. They had caused the Corporation a series of major headaches. And despite the best efforts of his Chief of Peace, General Decimal, the Chairman had yet to identify and dispense with the culprits.

At least where he was presently headed – out on the far-flung planet of Kasteesh – there was no chance that his activities would be sabotaged by those meddling armour-clad barbarians. He had left the management of Earth's capital in the capable hands of his sister, Lanista. Perhaps by his return she would have resolved the Armouron problem.

The Chairman clicked his fingers for his drink to be topped up, and helped himself to another handful of snacks. *Yes*, he thought, a little time spent away from the office, terrorizing a whole new group of people, and perhaps an alien or two, was just the break he needed . . .

# Chapter 10
## Hoshiko's Daughter

Snow was beginning to get the hang of it now. Although it still felt totally weird to be conducting a conversation without speech, with each attempt she was finding it a little easier to form and transmit her mind-messages.

*So, where is the knight who lives among you now?* she asked Ko'Drall.

Her brain was buzzing with all the information the creatures had already fed into it. When they had discovered Snow shared their gift of telepathy, their attitude had become more welcoming. And once *she* had grasped that they meant her no harm and appeared to be somehow connected to her own order, Snow had bombarded them with

103

questions: Who were they? What was this place? How did the Armouron fit in?

Ko'Drall and his comrades had waited patiently as she struggled to ask all this telepathically, then answered each question as best they could. Before long, Snow had grasped a basic understanding of her situation and of the creatures' ancient relationship with the Armouron Knights.

*There is no longer a Rider among us, I fear*, Ko'Drall told her in answer to her latest question. His tone was grim. *Some twenty cycles ago, a new force arrived on our planet. Many Wingless ones and their army of Void slaves. They attacked our colony, destroying much of it completely and killing many of our number.*

Snow could sense the deep sadness in Ko'Drall and his fellow creatures. It wasn't difficult to guess who the destructive 'new force' were. The Corporation. 'Void slaves' was a good description of the Chairman's mindless, merciless White Knight troops.

*Our Armouron comrade, the last Rider, fought more courageously than any to repel the invaders*, continued Ko'Drall. *He and his mind-mate Ja'Prith flew into battle over and over again, showing no fear. But the enemy's numbers were too great. In the end, both Ja'Prith and the brave Hoshiko were captured.*

*Hoshiko!* The sound of her father's name sent Snow's brain spinning. For a few moments, she was too bewildered and confused to form a response. Ko'Drall and the others watched her evident shock with puzzled alarm.

*Hoshiko was my father's name,* she told them simply, when she regained her composure.

*Your father!* Ko'Drall's surprise at the revelation was almost as great as hers. *Yes! Of course! That is why you have the ability to hear and speak with us, no doubt! Of all the Riders in our long history,* he explained, *Hoshiko formed the strongest mental link with his mind-mate. You share his skill.*

In the light of this astonishing discovery, Snow's brain was throwing up a whole host of new questions.

*What happened to him?* she asked. *After he and Ja'Prith were captured, I mean.*

*They were taken to the enemy stronghold from which you yourself escaped,* replied Ko'Drall. He bowed his long head sadly as he continued. *We have had no contact with them since.*

*So my father could still be alive!* thought Snow. *I could rescue him!*

Snow had not intended this last thought to be shared. But the creatures had heard. The one who had initially treated her with most suspicion, who she now knew was called Ly'Throk, gazed gravely at her.

*No. Do not cheat your heart so, child,* he told her gently. *Those who command the Void Ones rarely keep their prisoners alive. And we have tried many times, without success, to penetrate the enemy's base. There is a barrier around it that neither we, nor our mind-messages, can penetrate.*

*My brother is right, Hoshiko's daughter,* agreed Ko'Drall. *You saw for yourself how I was struck down by the stronghold's invisible shield.* He looked at her tenderly. *And it is highly improbable that Ja'Prith and your father are still alive, after all this time.*

Snow remembered the voice that had cried out in her mind, back at the Academy. The voice that had come from the canister with which she had been brought to this alien place.

*But they might be,* she replied with spirit. Her eyes burned with grim determination.

*And if they are,* she continued, *I'm going to get them out.*

## Chapter 11
### Arrivals

Dr Grinkov was on the verge of breaking into a nervous sweat. It was some time since he had met the Chairman face to face. But he hadn't forgotten the experience.

Why, oh why, had there had to be a security breach in this, of all weeks? The research station usually ran like clockwork. Months passed without incident. But yesterday – only the day before the Chairman was to begin his first visit to Kasteesh in over a year – the station had had to deal with an intruder alert *and* an attack by one of the planet's native creatures. Fortunately, the executive shuttle hadn't arrived until things had calmed down.

Grinkov anxiously watched the boarding ramp extend from the shuttle's hatch to the hangar floor. He mopped his brow.

*It'll be OK*, the Head of Operations told himself. *Just tell him about it quickly, then move on to something else.*

His uneasiness was worsened by the fact that the Chairman already seemed displeased with him. When the doctor had received a vidcom message from the Corporation boss informing him that the sickly Mshanga prisoner was being sent back to Kasteesh, it was clear that the Chairman held Grinkov to blame for the creature's ill-health, which was hardly fair.

The shuttle's hatch-seal popped with a hiss and its door began to slide to one side.

*Just don't make him any more angry, that's the key*, thought the nervous scientist. He knew only too well how important it was to stay in the Chairman's good books. Grinkov was the station's sixth Head of Operations in three years. His predecessors had all disappointed their superior in some way. None had been seen since being relieved of their duties.

The doctor watched the familiar short, plump

figure descend the ramp, flanked by his White Knight bodyguard. As he approached, the Chairman acknowledged him with a haughty nod.

'Grinkov.'

'Welcome to Kasteesh, Chairman.'

'The Mshanga brute arrived alive, I trust?'

'Yes, sir. The prisoner has been returned to the laboratory. It is already showing signs of recovery.'

The Chairman snorted.

'Not that I care whether the beast lives or dies, you understand,' he said. 'But since the wretched creature has proved to be a wash-out as an Arena attraction, I'd like to get *some* other use out of it.'

'Quite, sir,' said Grinkov. 'If you remember, sir, I did advise you that the creature could find Earth's atmosphere unsuitable for its—'

'I've no time for excuses, Grinkov,' snarled the Chairman. 'I've decided to continue our investigations into the beast's unusual brain-function. If these Mshanga can exhibit mind-powers, I'm determined the Corporation will have them too.'

'Absolutely, sir,' nodded Grinkov. 'Is it your

desire to restart the experiments right now, sir?'

'It is. I'll observe the first trials myself. So find a new human mind-partner for the beast, Doctor.' He gave the scientist a withering look. 'And quickly!'

As the Chairman made to move off, Grinkov cleared his throat uncomfortably.

'Er, there is *one* other thing, Chairman . . .'

'Yes?'

'When our technicians unloaded the creature, they discovered a stowaway, sir, inside the cargo pod.'

'And where is this stowaway now?' asked the Chairman wearily.

'Our security officers chased the intruder from the premises, sir. The child was regrettably snatched by one of the alien beasts.'

'A *child*, you say?'

'Yes, Chairman, we believe so. Although it was hard to be certain, because the intruder was wearing a helmet.'

The colour drained from the Chairman's face.

'And armour?' he hissed.

'No, sir,' replied the doctor, looking rather puzzled. 'No armour, sir.'

For a moment or two, the Chairman seemed lost in anxious thought.

'Of course not . . .' he muttered under his breath. 'It couldn't be . . . Not right out here . . . Still . . .' He spoke sharply to Grinkov again. 'Double the security patrols!' he snapped. 'If this intruder should somehow find their way back into the facility, I want them neutralized on sight! Understood?'

'Yes, sir. Absolutely, sir.'

As the executive party moved off, Dr Grinkov discreetly let out a long sigh of relief.

*That could have been worse, I suppose*, he thought. He felt hopeful that with a bit of luck and a lot of schmoozing on his part, the Chairman would find the rest of his visit to his satisfaction.

Just as long as nothing *else* went wrong.

The elevator's doors hissed open and the White Knight captain strode purposefully through them into the quarantine area. As it had instructed, a team of four other android security officers were already standing guard around the suspect cargo pod. The captain approached the one with the red shoulder flash.

'Report in full, Sergeant.'

'Yes, Captain. This unidentified pod was unloaded eleven minutes ago from the hold of the Chairman's executive shuttle. It does not appear on the ship's inventory file.'

'Have you checked its details with Nu-Topia control?'

'Yes, Captain. Their systems found a match for its identity code. The pod was registered for dispatch to the penal compound on the ice planet Festol II. The ship on which it was scheduled to be loaded has yet to depart Nu-Topia, sir.'

'Did their records specify its contents?'

'Yes, sir. Twelve tonnes of canned soya meat. Sled-dog food, sir.'

The captain's logic circuits analysed the information. They calculated that there was a very high probability – over ninety per cent – that the pod's inclusion in the shuttle's cargo was a simple mix-up. It was almost certainly due to a faulty tag. Normally, the robot officer would have ordered the misdirected pod to be sent back on the next ship to Nu-Topia and left it at that.

But the captain had been given a clear directive from the station's Head of Operations only minutes earlier. While the Chairman was on site, security was to be watertight. Anything out of the ordinary, however insignificant, was to be investigated.

'Open the pod up, Sergeant. Conduct a thorough search of its contents.'

'Yes, sir!'

The sergeant passed on the order to the three android constables, who quickly disabled the cargo pod's seals and activated its opening mechanism. The pod's edges slowly parted as its sides began to fold down.

One of the White Knight constables suddenly clutched at its neck. A shower of sparks sprayed out between its metal fingers. A slim crossbow bolt was lodged in the android's throat. As its primary circuits shorted out, the White Knight slumped to the floor.

Rake burst from the opening pod, brandishing his shortsword. He took a scything swing at a second White Knight before it could react to its comrade's collapse. It too went down.

Rake's fellow Armouron were right behind him. Tea-Leaf, Hoax and Oddball all leaped from within the pod. Tea-Leaf already had her bow

re-loaded. She launched her second bolt at the remaining constable. The android dodged to one side – only to step straight into a knockout blow from Oddball's heavy warhammer.

Hoax had his sights on the sergeant. As the White Knight hurriedly unsheathed its weapon, Hoax planted one end of his fighting staff on the floor and leaped at the guard, pole-vault style. He landed a fierce two-footed kick in the android's metal midriff, sending it sprawling. Twirling his staff gleefully, Hoax quickly moved in to finish the job.

The only android still standing was the White

Knight captain. Rake saw it reach for its throat-mounted comlink, to call for backup. In one swift motion he extended his sword into spear mode and launched it at the armoured robot. The spear skewered it straight through its comlink. It clattered to the floor, then lay still, its wrecked voice-synthesizer emitting a continuous high-pitched whistle.

Hoax, who had now dealt with the android sergeant, looked up and grinned.

'Hey, guys – kettle's boiling!'

But Salt, who had just stepped out from the cargo pod, wasn't amused.

'Shut that thing up!' he growled. 'Before it draws attention.'

Oddball stepped up to oblige, silencing the electronic screech with a hammer blow.

Salt looked around at the fallen robot guards and grunted.

'Hmph. Good work, all of you,' he said gruffly. 'Now, get this scrap metal cleared up, quickly.' He nodded to the cargo pod. 'Dump them in there. We'll seal it again. The longer we delay their discovery, the better.'

As the four young knights carried out his

instructions, Salt limped over to a bank of vidcam monitors mounted on the far wall. They showed various views of the main hangar. On one screen, he could see a clear view of the executive shuttle, now being serviced by a team of robot cleaners. Another showed the opposite side of the hangar, where a much larger ship stood unattended – presumably the freight transporter in which Alida had left Nu-Topia.

Salt's students joined him.

'All tidy, master,' said Rake. 'And we've resealed the pod. What next?'

'Next,' replied the old armourer, 'we find Alida. I want the four of you to search the compound.'

'Should we split up?' asked Tea-Leaf.

'I think not, in this instance,' replied Salt. 'Stay together. But only engage the guards if absolutely necessary.'

He looked back at the image of the freight ship on the vidcam screen.

'I, in the meantime, will procure us transport for our return to Earth.'

'You're gonna pinch that freighter?' said Hoax. 'Without your armour? What happens if you're seen?'

'I shall make it my business not to be,' rumbled Salt. 'As soon as you have found Alida, meet me at the ship. Now – *go!*'

He watched his team dash for the elevator then disappear behind its sliding doors. Moving with remarkable stealth for a big man with a damaged leg, he made his own way towards the area's other exit.

## Chapter 12
### Through the Pain Barrier

Snow's second air-lift in the grip of Ko'Drall's claws was less hair-raising than the first – if only because she knew now that he was a friend, not a foe. Nevertheless, as the huge beast gently placed her back on the ground, close to the spot where they had first met, she was relieved to feel the rock beneath her feet.

Ko'Drall settled beside her and together they surveyed the scene of his recent battle. The battered robotic bodies of the three White Knights he had put out of action were still lying on the dusty ground where they had fallen.

Snow knew that just beyond them was the invisible barrier that had caused her so much pain when she had unknowingly run into it.

*Are you sure you want to go through with this, child?* asked Ko'Drall's mind-voice. *None of my own race has yet to penetrate the barrier. Its effect on you when you passed through it was severe. A second time could be fatal.*

*I'll be fine*, replied Snow, as much to convince herself as her new-found ally. *It'll hurt, I know, but I'll get over it. It's the only way I can get back inside the compound.*

To do that, there was something else she needed. She hurried to the nearest of the robot bodies. Its armoured metal torso lay face down. A little distance away, its severed head stared blankly skywards.

Snow rolled the lifeless android over.

*Yes!*

As she had hoped, the White Knight had a security keycard clipped to its belt. Snow grabbed it eagerly.

*OK, I'm ready.* She turned to look at Ko'Drall. *You remember what we agreed?*

The creature held her gaze with its strange yellow eyes. *Yes, Hoshiko's daughter. If you succeed in bringing down the barrier, you will send us a signal.*

*I and my kin will then attack the invaders' stronghold in force.*

The war-party had already been gathering as they left the colony – around thirty or so of the huge, silent creatures. Ly'Throk had told Snow these were the only remaining survivors of the Corporation's brutal invasion. Snow's plan was their last hope of freeing their home world from the Chairman's cruel rule.

*I'd best get on with it then*, thought Snow.

She turned towards the compound, trying to ignore the fear rising from her stomach and summon the courage for what she had to do next. She drew in a long, slow breath through her helmet's filters.

It was her helmet, she hoped, that would make all the difference.

Whatever the invisible barrier around the research station was, it was clearly designed to affect those whose minds were sensitive to psychic transmissions. The telepathic creatures could not bear to come into contact with it. It had caused Snow such great pain for the same reason.

But it hadn't blocked her completely, as it had Ko'Drall's kind. She had been able to break through. Snow was convinced this could only be due to her helmet. It had shielded her mind from the full effects of the anti-psychic force field, she felt sure – just as sure as she now was that it had been her helmet which had amplified that first telepathic voice, back at the Academy.

The knowledge that the helmet Salt had crafted for her seemed to be both focusing and shielding her apparent psychic sensitivity threw up all sorts of confusing questions in Snow's mind. Had Salt already known of her telepathic ability, before she did? If so, how? And why hadn't he told her?

But for now, it was enough to know that the helmet had helped her get past the force field. And it would do so again, she hoped.

She still needed to draw on all the bravery of an Armouron Knight, though, to face that pain again.

*Wish me luck, Ko'Drall.*

The creature bowed its alien head. *Go well, my friend.*

Snow took a few strides backwards, then set off at a dash towards the research station. She sprinted past the scattered remains of the White Knights, then –

*Aaaaaaarrrrrrgggghhh!!!*

Snow staggered, then stumbled, then fell heavily, as the pain exploded in her mind. She tore her tunic and skinned her knees and palms as she hit the rocky ground.

Stranded on the other side of the invisible barrier, Ko'Drall watched, his eyes full of sympathy and concern, as Snow lay sprawled in the dust, panting.

Several minutes passed before Snow eventually struggled to her feet. She turned back towards her friend. Despite her injuries and her obvious pallor, she managed a half-smile. *I'm OK.*

No answer came. Snow remembered that her friend could no longer hear her, nor send her his thoughts. The anti-psychic barrier was blocking their telepathic communication.

She gave Ko'Drall a reassuring wave, then turned her attention to the research station behind her. The emergency exit through which she had originally fled the compound was nearby. Snow stooped to pick up the keycard – she had dropped it when she fell – then made her way towards the door.

She was on her own again now.

# Chapter 13
## Cause for Concern

'What do you mean, *missing*?' snarled the Chairman. 'How can a squad of five guards just go *missing*?'

The Chairman was seated behind Dr Grinkov's expansive desk. He had commandeered the head scientist's office for the duration of his visit. He had been happily doodling a design for a new robotic beast for the Arena when the White Knight captain arrived with its worrying report.

'The unit last checked in at eleven seventeen hours,' replied the android impassively. 'They were assigned a security task in the quarantine area. They have failed to contact Control since.'

'And have you *looked* for them?' snapped the

Corporation boss impatiently.

'Yes, sir. There is no sign of them in the quarantine area or anywhere else in the compound. But one of the search team did find this.' The White Knight placed something slim and metallic, about ten centimetres long, on the desktop.

The Chairman's eyes narrowed into a scowl, as he looked at the mystery object. He had seen something identical to this only recently, buried in the wrecked body of one of his White Knights following a raid on a Corporation field generator. It was a bolt from a crossbow. Only an Armouron Knight would use such an antiquated weapon.

The Chairman lifted his livid face to the android officer.

'I want a repeat search conducted immediately!' he spat. 'And this time, don't report back until you can tell me what happened to those guards!'

'Yes, sir.'

'And, Captain . . .' the Chairman added as the Knight turned to leave. 'Make sure my shuttle is refuelled and on standby for lift-off, as a matter of priority!'

The Kasteesh outpost had a garrison of several hundred White Knights. Even if an enemy of the

Corporation had somehow managed to infiltrate the compound, there were more than enough guards to deal with them.

But in the Chairman's experience, it always paid to be ready to make a swift exit.

Just to be on the safe side.

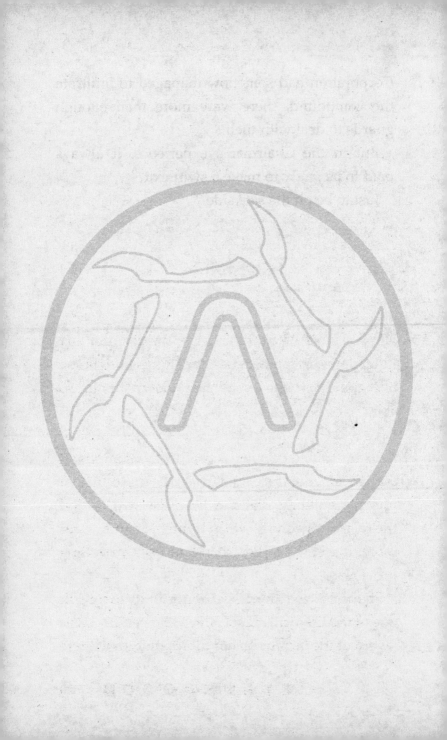

# Chapter 14
## Charge of the Knight Brigade

Snow sprinted round a bend in the corridor, her heart pounding in her chest, her lungs fit to burst. She couldn't believe she had blown things so soon.

The keycard had worked a treat – she had had no trouble gaining access to the compound via the emergency exit. But as she stole further into the building, she had been alarmed to find the place swarming with White Knights – far more, it seemed to her, than had been patrolling previously.

She had seized the earliest opportunity to consult one of the fire-drill maps, which showed the basic layout of the facility. To her disappointment, there was no obvious area in which to look for Ja'Prith and her father. Various sectors of the map were unlabelled. Perhaps the prisoners were in one of these.

The force-field generator wasn't marked either. If Ly'Throk's war-party were to have a chance of attacking the Corporation base, Snow needed to find that generator and put it out of operation.

But even as she moved off, with this purpose in mind, a White Knight constable had spotted her and raised the alarm. Now there were at least a dozen of the android security guards hot on her tail.

As Snow hared along the corridor, running for her life, the White Knights rounded the corner behind her. Several fired their blasters as they ran.

*It's just like the PShooter test*, Snow tried to tell herself, as she ducked and wove, desperate to evade the crackling red bolts of energy. Only this time, she had no armour. And she wasn't dodging harmless ball-bearings.

She skidded into another side passage and began tearing along it. Then her heart sank. Twenty metres ahead, a light was flashing in the corridor ceiling. A pair of security doors were slicing closed across the passageway, sealing it off.

She was trapped.

She reached the sealed doors as the pursuing White Knights came storming into the passageway. When they saw Snow standing helpless, her back against a dead-end, they slowed their pace. They came to a halt a few metres away. At their captain's order, they raised their blasters and took careful aim.

'ARMOURON!!!'

For a moment, Snow thought she had lost the plot. Four armour-clad figures had just come tearing round the corner into the corridor and were charging down the White Knights from behind, bellowing ferociously.

It *couldn't* be . . .

But it was.

Rake, Tea-Leaf, Oddball and Hoax, in full-blown battle-mode. They ploughed into the surprised androids like a living tsunami.

Rake's first vicious sword-stroke severed one android's forearm, sending its blaster skittering across the floor. He whirled round, red armour

flashing, to deliver a second slicing blow. This one took the robot's head clean off. Its mechanical torso, with cables spewing from its neck, staggered away, to collide with the corridor wall.

Hoax had already floored two enemies with sweeping strikes of his fighting staff. He jabbed the staff's tip hard into the eye-cam of a third android. As it staggered backwards, Hoax snapped the staff into two shorter chain-linked sections – his nunchaku. His wrists became a blur as he delivered a lightning-fast sequence of whiplash blows to his enemy's neck and head. Sparks flew from the White Knight's punctured eye as it dropped to the floor, its systems wrecked.

Another android aimed a powerful kick at Hoax from behind. It hadn't bargained on his unique orange armour. The suit's ingeniously sprung backplate absorbed much of the kick's force, then reflected it along the robot's own leg. The jolt was enough to blow the servos in its hip. It tottered and fell.

Tea-Leaf's crossbow was little use at such close quarters. Instead, she had unsheathed the dagger concealed in its stock. Although the White Knights' armour was designed to be impenetrable, Tea-Leaf knew otherwise. There were one or two vulnerable areas where a fierce, precise stab could do untold damage to the androids' internal electronics. Her keen reflexes and ultra-light suit helped her dodge about until she saw her chance to strike. She had already put down two enemies and now lunged at a third.

Oddball's approach was a little less subtle, but equally effective. A no-nonsense body-blow from his hefty warhammer sent another of the White Knights sprawling.

The fight raged on, the young Armouron

cutting down androids with one expert move after another. Soon, there were only two left standing. Hoax swept the legs out from under one of them with a low reverse roundhouse kick. Oddball thumped down his hammer to crush the stricken robot's central processor. The last android was brought down by combined strikes from Tea-Leaf and Rake's flashing blades.

All at once, the din of battle ceased. The corridor fell silent.

The four young knights straightened up, breathing heavily, surrounded by a sea of white bodies. As Rake and Tea-Leaf sheathed their weapons, Hoax twirled his nunchaku nonchalantly, grinning.

'That was fun!'

Oddball gave him a wry smile. 'Glad you enjoyed it, 'cos there'll be plenty more.' He pointed to the flashing ceiling light. 'The alarm's still going.'

Rake spoke urgently to Tea-Leaf. 'Can you look out for the next lot?'

Tea-Leaf nodded. She turned to watch the open end of the corridor, her crossbow raised and ready.

✹ ❦ ⬩ ● ◉ Ⓐ ⬤ ◈ ◯ ✦

The others gathered around Snow.

'Are you OK?' asked Oddball.

Snow nodded silently. 'How did you find me?' she asked incredulously. It felt odd to use actual speech, not her mind-voice, for the first time in a while.

'Long story,' replied Rake. 'And it'll have to wait. Right now, we need to get out of here. There'll be plenty of time to catch up on the way home.'

His tone became rather sharp.

'Then maybe you can explain why you didn't tell the rest of us you were planning a little off-world jaunt.'

Snow looked hurt. 'I didn't plan *any* of this, Rake!' she protested.

Rake looked into his friend's pale, drawn face. Snow looked tired and frightened.

'Anyway, we've got something for you,' he said more warmly. He looked at her grazed knees and torn tunic. 'Although it looks like you could have done with it sooner.' He nodded to Oddball.

'Here you go!' Oddball unslung the pack from his shoulder and dumped it at Snow's feet. He flashed her a smile. 'Helmet-only isn't a good look for you, to be honest.'

Snow's eyes lit up as she pulled her blue Armouron breastplate from the pack. Her full suit, her shield and her tonfa were all inside. She smiled her thanks and hurriedly began to put on the armour.

Rake watched her take her medallion from her tunic and snap it into her breastplate. Armour-clad, she looked much more her old self.

'Ready?' he asked. 'Then let's get back to the hangar while we still can. Hopefully, Salt's got that freighter all set to take us home.'

But as he turned to lead the way, Snow grabbed his arm.

'There's something I have to do before we can leave!'

'What?'

'I promised to help someone. Friends of the order.'

'The Mshanga?' asked Oddball.

Snow gave him a blank look. It wasn't a name she had heard.

'Whopping great flying things,' added Hoax.

So they knew about the creatures. There was no time to ask how.

'Yes. The Corporation have devastated their colony. I promised them I'd take out the force field around this compound, so they can fight back,' Snow explained. 'I was looking for the shield generator when the guards spotted me.'

'I know where it is,' said Oddball. 'Do you remember that area we searched with the bank of gas-cooled wave-stabilizing units, guys?'

The others looked at him.

'What?' he said defensively. 'Some of us notice these things!'

Hoax shook his head despairingly.

'Anyway,' continued Oddball. 'Those units could only be part of a field transmission system. That's your shield generator.'

Rake turned back to Snow.

'So – if we take out the shield, *then* can we get out of here?'

'They've got one of the creatures locked up in here,' said Snow. For some reason, she chose not to mention her hopes of finding a second prisoner. 'If you knock out the generator, I'll free the captive creature.'

Rake blew out his cheeks. 'The old man told us to get you out of here, plain and simple. He'll kill me if he finds out I let you go off on your own again.' He gave a grim smile. 'That is, if any of us get out of this mess alive.'

He looked into Snow's pleading eyes. He could sense this meant a lot to her. Maybe the prisoner was a friend of her father's. And Salt *had* told them the Mshanga were ancient allies of their order . . .

Tea-Leaf suddenly gave an urgent shout. 'We've got company!' Her ultra-sensitive hearing had picked up the sound of an approaching party. 'At least twenty Kettles, coming our way fast!'

Rake reached a decision.

'OK, Snow, we do it your way,' he said determinedly. 'We'll deal with this next bunch together, then split up. You find your prisoner. The rest of us will put the generator out of operation and keep the guards busy. Get back to the hangar as soon as you can.'

Snow nodded gratefully.

By now, they could all hear the thuds of running feet. The guards were almost upon them.

Rake drew his sword.

'Right, then – who fancies a bit more Kettle-bashing?'

The others readied their weapons too. Snow took firm hold of her tonfa and shield, happy to have them in her grasp once again.

'Stand Together!' yelled Hoax.

'Battle as One!' four voices cried in unison.

As a wave of white-armoured bodies came flooding round the corner, the young knights charged to meet them.

## Chapter 15
### The Prisoner

Snow decided to give it one last try. She could think of no other way to find them. She couldn't search the entire compound, with so many guards on the lookout. This *had* to work.

She calmed her mind, then formed the message again.

*Ja'Prith? Father? Can you hear me?*

It had been hard enough getting the hang of using her telepathy at close quarters. She didn't even know if she had the ability to make mind-contact over a greater distance. But it was her only hope.

She waited. As seconds passed, her heart began to sink. Then –

*Who calls my name?*

Snow recognized the mind-voice immediately, though its tone was far calmer than the last time she had heard it, back at the Academy.

*A friend*, she replied. *I wish to help you. Can you guide me to where you are?*

There was a long pause.

*I can.*

Snow had expected to receive directions, or a description of the creature's whereabouts. What she got was far more straightforward. She suddenly knew, with absolute certainty, which route to take.

She made her way swiftly along one corridor after another, guided by the sure sense of direction which Ja'Prith was somehow planting in her mind. Her route quickly led her to an area on the opposite side of the compound to the hangar. The gentle pull on her mind stopped as she silently approached a silver door. There were White Knight sentries posted on either side of it.

Grasping her combat baton firmly, Snow sprang from cover.

She had both the element of surprise and her intensive Armouron training on her side. The android guards never stood a chance. Seconds later, they lay beside one another on the corridor floor, twitching and sparking.

Snow swiped her stolen keycard across the door sensor and it hissed open. She stepped forward into a large, low-ceilinged laboratory room.

And there was Ja'Prith. Snow's first sight of the creature sent a powerful surge of pity and anger through her mind.

The huge beast was being held behind a thick, transparent wall. He was lying face down on the laboratory floor, surrounded by banks of scientific equipment.

In size and form, Ja'Prith was much like the other creatures from the Kasteesh colony. But his body had been horribly abused by his Corporation captors. His elegant head-crest was threaded with electronic sensors and wiring. Areas of his stone-plated hide had been cut away or punctured, to allow for the attachment of electrodes. His short hind legs, which he was forced by his unnatural position to stretch out behind him, had been brutally sheared of their claws, such that they now appeared useless.

Worst of all was the method by which he had

been restrained. His wings had been pinioned to the laboratory floor. A pair of crackling blue plasma-shackles held them stretched flat, so that the noble beast could only raise his elongated head, with difficulty, but was otherwise completely immobilized.

Ja'Prith's great yellow eyes met Snow's pitying gaze.

*You are much like your father, little Wingless One.*

Snow was taken aback. She had expected to have to introduce herself.

*How do you know who I am?*

*Your mind, as much as your physical form, mirror his,* came the reply. *You are Hoshiko's daughter.*

There was a pause, then –

*I sense that you had hoped to find your father with me.*

It was true. As much as Snow was pleased to have located Ja'Prith, her overriding sensation was one of bitter disappointment.

*Do you know what happened to him?* she asked.

Ja'Prith's eyes seemed to cloud with pain. It was a few moments before his response came.

*When your father and I fell in battle, we were both brought to this dreadful place. For many months, the white-coats conducted tests and experiments on us both.*

*The experiments were terrible. They caused us both great pain. In your father's case, they did untold damage. But they were successful, in their way. They unlocked areas of your father's unique mind that he had never accessed before. He began to exhibit even greater psychic abilities — ones that our enemies craved.*

*One day, your father was taken from our cell. That was the last time I saw him.*

Snow could sense the desolation in Ja'Prith's mind-voice. The separation had clearly hurt him deeply.

*I tried endlessly to reach his mind, but without success. I learned later that he had been transported to Earth, for further experimentation.*

*Then recently, after all this time,* he continued, *I too was taken to Earth by my captors. I hoped desperately to be reunited with your father. I put my life's energy, night and day, into generating the most powerful mind-call I could, in the hope of reaching him.*

*I heard you,* Snow told Ja'Prith. *Only I didn't know how to respond then.*

*The effort made me weak,* the creature went on. *And before long, I found myself back in this cursed cell—*

The floor suddenly juddered violently beneath Snow's feet. The sound of a massive explosion followed a split second later.

Snow knew instinctively that the tremor was due to Oddball's handiwork – a detonation big enough to put several shield generators out of action.

'Yes!' she cried, out loud. 'They did it!'

Hopefully, Ko'Drall would have seen the explosion and realized what it meant. But it was better to be sure.

*My friends have disabled the shield that protects the compound*, Snow explained hurriedly to Ja'Prith. *I told your comrades that I'd send a signal, once the shield was down. But I'm not sure I have the mind-strength to call them from so far. Can you?*

The giant creature's eyes blazed brightly.

*It is already done, my friend.*

A moment later, Snow's mind filled with a multitude of voices – the answering mind-cries of Ly'Throk, Ko'Drall and their fellow creatures.

*We come, dear brother! We come, Hoshiko's daughter! We come!*

'Come *on*, Snow!' Rake muttered through clenched teeth. 'Where *are* you?'

He was standing beside Tea-Leaf and Hoax at the foot of the freighter's boarding ramp. His eyes glanced eagerly from the opening of one corridor to the next, desperate to see the figure of Snow appear along one of them.

Even if she did show up, she was going to have a job getting to the ship. A host of White Knights had formed a semi-circle around its ramp and were slowly closing in. Only the steady stream of crossbow bolts that Tea-Leaf was sending their way, combined with Hoax's barrage of well-aimed flash-bang pellets, were keeping them at bay.

After they had separated from Snow, they had managed to fulfil their part of the bargain – to take out the psychic shield – without too much difficulty. Once they had dealt with the White Knight guards in the shield generator area, Oddball had taken great pleasure in blowing its main power cell sky high.

With the shield out of action, they had fought their way back to the freight ship. They found Salt waiting anxiously for them. But there was no sign of Snow.

Oddball appeared at the top of the ramp. His typically bright-eyed expression had given way to a look of grim despair.

'The old man says we can't wait any longer,' he yelled flatly. 'The Mshanga attack is starting to bring the building down. If we don't leave now, he's worried we won't get out at all.'

Rake didn't reply. He could hear for himself the violent thuds, crashes and protesting groans that were evidence of the creatures' fierce onslaught against the roof and walls of the compound. It had begun only minutes after they had knocked out the shield and had continued relentlessly since. The building wouldn't stand much more.

Tea-Leaf, still firing off bolts desperately, shouted over the din, 'He's right, Rake.' Her face was as bleak as Oddball's. 'We have to go. Maybe Snow got out some other way. She might be OK.'

Rake knew she didn't believe that any more than he did.

Hoax pulled another handful of red pellets from the compartment in his leg guard and hurled them at the front rank of White Knights. They exploded in a burst of noise and coloured smoke. He delved in the compartment again – then held up his empty hands to Rake.

'I'm out!'

Tea-Leaf loosed a final shot, then lowered her bow.

'Me too,' she said grimly.

Rake's expression was desolate. This wasn't

how their rescue mission was supposed to end.
He had come to Kasteesh to bring Snow home.

But they had no choice.

'OK. Fall back,' he cried. 'We're leaving.'

As his fellow knights made their way up the
ramp, Rake turned to follow. He cast one last
backward glance at the hangar.

'Sorry, Snow,' he murmured.

Then he leaped onto the already rising ramp
and hurried into the belly of the ship.

## Chapter 16
### Abandoned Ship

'Captain!' yelled the Chairman angrily. 'CAPTAIN!' The Corporation boss was purple-faced and wild-eyed. 'Get this ship out of here at once, do you hear me? AT ONCE!!'

The Chairman was sitting bolt upright in his personal lounger chair in the deserted flight cabin of his executive spacecraft. He had a rather petulant, spoiled-child look, as though he couldn't quite grasp the idea that nobody was paying attention to his demands.

He knew where everyone was. The shuttle's entire crew – White Knights and human technicians and officers alike – were outside in the hangar, fighting a losing battle against

Kasteesh's fearsome natives.

The Chairman had been anxiously watching the battle unfold through the cabin's viewport. A dozen of the alien creatures had now gained entry to the compound. They were advancing fearlessly across the hangar floor, lurching forward on their wing-knuckles, scattering Corporation troops and scientists before them.

The creatures' advance was made all the more unnerving by the fact that they fought in silence. There were no alien war-cries, howls or screeches. Not that the battle wasn't noisy. As well as the yells of the Corporation fighters and the blasts of their laser fire, there were the resounding thumps and crashes against the hangar roof. The creatures' airborne comrades were battering the building's exterior with rock missiles dropped from their claws.

The Chairman couldn't believe this was happening. Not again. Not here.

*I build a secret outpost, clack knows how many light years from anywhere,* he thought furiously, *and those blasted fancy-armour-wearing do-gooders still manage to turn up and ruin things!*

He knew all too well that the Armouron were

to blame for his present predicament. He had seen them himself as he fled to his ship when the creatures' attack first began – a group of armoured figures fighting off White Knights as though their little band was a force of forty, not four. He had little doubt that they were somehow responsible for rallying the Mshanga into battle.

*They don't even look like adults!* raved the Chairman silently to himself. *Just four juvenile, jumped-up, interfering—*

His thoughts were interrupted by the arrival of one of his human officers. She looked battle-scarred and breathless. She hastily threw down the damaged blaster she was carrying and hurried to the cabin's weapon rack to grab a replacement.

The Chairman sprang from his lounger to intercept her.

'Officer! Can you fly this ship?'

The woman pulled up short, looking rather taken aback.

'Er . . . yes, sir . . . I completed my star-pilot training last year . . .'

'Thank Jupiter's moons!' shrieked the Chairman. 'Then get us out of this nightmare immediately!'

The woman's puzzled look deepened. She

seemed uncertain she had heard correctly.

'What are you waiting for, woman! That's an order!' raged the Chairman. 'Take off this instant!'

'But . . . sir . . .' she stuttered. 'What about the others?' She gestured towards the viewport and the battle raging outside. 'The compound is under attack. Its staff are fighting for their lives . . .'

'I don't care about them, you fool!' shrieked the Chairman, eyes bulging. 'This is about me! It's *always* about me!'

Suddenly, there was an almighty crash. One of the curving metal beams supporting the hangar roof had collapsed under the Mshanga's fierce barrage. A section of roof came tumbling down onto the bow end of the shuttle. The Chairman dived for cover as several large fragments burst through the cabin's shell and smashed down onto the flight consoles, sending up a shower of debris and sparks.

By the time he picked himself off the floor, the Chairman found the female officer gone. One look at the ruptured cabin roof and mangled control consoles told him that this ship was going nowhere soon.

There was the thud and scrape of something heavy settling on top of what remained of the cabin. A huge, elongated head thrust its way through the tear in the roof. Its yellow eyes scanned the cabin's interior and settled on the terrified Corporation boss.

The Chairman backed away in wide-eyed terror. He reached the narrow passageway that led towards the shuttle's aft, turned and fled. As he ran, in blind panic, he muttered frantically to himself, 'Must escape! Must escape! Must escape!'

Escape! That was it! The escape capsules!

The shuttle was fitted with several single-seater emergency escape capsules. In the event of the shuttle being struck by a meteor, or some other such catastrophe, human crew-members were able to eject and await rescue.

Fortunately for the Chairman, the capsules were situated in the ship's rear. He hurried to the first capsule's tiny hatch, squirmed his way through and sealed it behind him.

The capsule was intended for use in deep space, the Chairman knew. Exactly what would happen if he launched it while the shuttle was docked, he was not sure. But any misgivings he had were driven from his mind by the appearance of a second terrifying alien face, pressed up against the capsule's external viewport.

Shaking with fear, the Chairman struggled into the cramped capsule's single seat, strapped himself in and hit the launch button.

## Chapter 17
### The Last Rider

Snow's rescue plans had only ever extended as far as finding the imprisoned creature. She had never imagined that setting Ja'Prith free would prove to be the hard part. Nor had it occurred to her that once his fellow creatures had begun their siege of the research station, it would become such a very dangerous place to be.

But she was rapidly realizing this was the case. As she paced the floor, racking her brains for some way to liberate her father's mind-mate from his bonds, the structure of the building trembled and shook around her. If they didn't get out soon, they would be buried in the rubble along with their Corporation enemies.

She had tried everything she could think of to break through the transparent wall that enclosed Ja'Prith. She could make no impact on it with either her tonfa or her shield, though she had attacked it with all her might. There was a sensor in the wall, which she felt sure must cause the barrier to retract. But swiping her keycard across it had no effect.

*There is one way you might free me.*

Snow's response to Ja'Prith's mind-message was to press herself against the transparent wall between them.

*How?!*

*As I have told you, the white-coats' experiments unlocked new psychic abilities buried in your father's mind. The most remarkable was his capacity to move objects with his will. As his offspring, it is possible that this power has passed to you.*

Snow's mind flashed back to the swerving PShooter shot. It was one of several occasions in her past when something physical seemed to have been affected by her thoughts. But even if she did share this telekinetic power of her father's, how could that help now?

Her gaze fell on the plasma-shackle control

console, on the other side of the transparent wall. Its main power switch was set to ON.

*With my wings free,* continued Ja'Prith, *I would have enough strength to break down these feeble walls.*

Snow felt the stirrings of renewed hope. Closing her eyes, she emptied her mind of distracting thoughts and tried to access the part of it that had willed the ball-bearing missile to swerve. She felt the Flow begin to radiate through her body from her medallion. She opened her eyes again and focused both them and her thoughts on the power switch, willing it to move.

She felt a momentary rush in the Flow and the switch clicked to OFF, as though flipped by an invisible hand.

As the plasma-shackles fizzled out, Snow's mind filled with Ja'Prith's jubilant mind-cry. Lifting his untethered wings, the huge creature reared up. His head and back burst through the roof of the cell as though it was sugar-paper. He shook his powerful shoulders violently to tear himself free of cables and sensors. A single blow from one mighty wing-tip shattered the transparent barrier.

The hole that Ja'Prith had smashed in the ceiling was large enough to offer him an aerial escape route. Snow didn't doubt that he could easily have lifted her to safety too, in the manner that Ko'Drall had carried her – if it wasn't for the cruel damage to his hind legs.

*You should go, quickly*, urged Snow. *Fly, before it is too late. I'll find a way to reach my friends*.

Even as she sent the mind-message, she knew it wasn't true. The building was begining to collapse around her. And even if she could make it to the hangar, the others would have left in the freighter by now, or otherwise perished themselves. But she was an Armouron. It had been her duty to rescue Ja'Prith – and if she did not herself survive, she knew she had acted well.

*I think not, little Wingless One*, came Ja'Prith's response. His yellow eyes burned with a new intensity now. *You will leave this place in the manner that befits you*.

Snow watched in puzzled incomprehension as the massive creature tucked his wings beneath him to crouch low before her on the cell's rubble-strewn floor . . .

* * *

On board the freight ship, the mood was dismal.

'It's my fault,' murmured Rake, stony-faced. 'I should never have let her go off on her own again.'

All four knights were mournfully watching the receding view of the research station, as the ship moved steadily away from the battle scene.

From their bird's-eye view, they could see the extent of the damage to the Corporation compound. The majority of its buildings had now been demolished, or were ablaze. Mshanga were still circling above, swooping low every now and then to renew their attack.

It seemed impossible that Snow could have survived such devastation. Even the fact that their old enemy, the Chairman, might also have perished in the attack offered no consolation.

'Look!' said Tea-Leaf abruptly. She was pointing out of the viewport, back towards the compound. The others followed her gaze and saw why.

One of the Mshanga had broken away from its circling comrades and was rapidly pursuing them.

'Master!' yelled Rake urgently.

Salt turned his hollow eyes from the ship's controls.

'What is it, Templer?'

'One of the creatures is attacking us! It must think that we're Corporation troops, making an escape!'

The massive creature's powerful wing-beats had already brought it close behind them. It swooped out of sight for a moment, then suddenly loomed up large in the viewport, flying directly alongside them.

Hoax let out a sudden whoop of delight. His three friends stared out of the viewport in utter, delighted disbelief.

A familiar figure in blue armour sat astride the great beast's broad neck, holding onto the trailing edge of its head-crest as it powered its way through the air.

As what they were seeing sank in, Rake and the others waved wildly at their friend. Snow returned the gesture, beaming from ear to ear.

It didn't take a telepath to know that right now, the only thoughts going through Snow's mind were ones of pure joy.

## Chapter 18
### Mayday

The tiny spherical escape capsule reached the top of its trajectory and began an arching dive back towards the rocky ground below. By the time it hit, it was falling fast. The impact crushed its foremost section flat. It bounced twice, spinning wildly, then ploughed across the planet's dusty surface and came to a groaning standstill.

Inside the battered capsule, the Chairman took several minutes to regain his sense of which way was up, which way down. The landing had shaken him about like a dried pea in a rattle. He was bruised and breathless – but alive.

The Chairman had always been blessed with remarkably good luck. Today was no exception.

Had he selected any one of the executive shuttle's other five escape capsules, he would almost certainly have been fired straight into the hangar's solid wall or floor. As it was, his tiny capsule had shot upwards, rocketing through the large rift that the Mshanga had made in the hangar roof.

When the capsule's systems had sensed its rapid descent, its tiny thrusters had fired bravely. But they were designed only to gently guide a free-floating space vehicle – not defy the pull of gravity. A crash-landing had been inevitable.

As his brain began to function properly again, the Chairman scanned the capsule's interior, and tried to decide on his next step. The exit hatch was quite clearly crushed beyond a hope of opening. So he was trapped inside.

Then he must call for help.

There was a small comlink handset clipped to the armrest of his seat. He snatched it and raised it to his mouth.

'Mayday, Mayday, this is an emergency.'

The Chairman depressed the comlink's main switch as he spoke, hoping this was the right thing to do. He wasn't used to having to work things for himself.

'Can anyone hear me? I repeat, this is an emergency.'

He released the switch and waited. Nothing happened.

Sweat beading on his pale forehead, the Chairman tried again.

'Mayday, Mayday. I am in need of urgent assistance. Please respond.'

This time, after a few seconds' delay, a faint voice came crackling from the handset's transducer.

'Distress call received loud and clear. This is the trade ship *Fatfox*. I hear you, friend. We have a location fix. Please identify yourself.'

The Chairman blew out his cheeks in relief, then squeezed the comlink again.

'Come and get me immediately.'

There was another short pause. Then the *Fatfox*'s answer came back.

'I repeat, please identify. Who am I speaking to?'

The Chairman was losing his patience. He squeezed the switch irritably.

'Don't you recognize my voice, you imbecile? This is the Chairman speaking, leader of the Perfect World.'

The pause this time was significantly longer. Then . . .

'Very funny, wise guy,' crackled the stranger's voice. 'And I'm Queen Tallulah of Neptune. Did you know that misuse of the Mayday distress call is a galactic offence? I suggest you try some other prank next time.'

The comlink went dead. Despite several attempts to raise the *Fatfox* again, the Chairman could get no response.

In a surge of temper, he flung the handset against the wall. It rattled around the tiny spherical escape pod, before coming to rest somewhere underneath his seat.

*This would never have happened if it wasn't for those infuriating Armouron!* thought the Chairman bitterly. His hatred for his old adversaries was growing with his rising sense of panic. *Wait till I get out of this mess. I'll make those armoured fools wish their precious order had never been formed!*

# Chapter 19
## Departures

Snow looked from Ja'Prith to the waiting ship and back again. The heaviness she felt in her heart showed in her face.

*Your fellow knights await you, my young friend. You must go.*

Her father's mind-mate stood before her in the odd M-shaped posture of his kind. His narrow eyes held a sadness too. But the voice Snow heard in her mind was calm and resolute.

*Even the best armour in the universe cannot stop some things hurting. Parting brings pain, but it will pass.*

Salt had put the freighter down on the planet's rocky surface as soon as he had realized that the creature pursuing them was carrying Snow. Ja'Prith had swooped down to settle beside the ship. All four knights had hurriedly disembarked to greet Snow – and her remarkable companion. It wasn't every day you got to meet a real-life alien, after all. Salt too had come to pay his respects to the giant beast.

Tea-Leaf, Rake and the others had wanted to hear all about Snow's narrow escape from the besieged research station. Snow had pointed out that, for a while at least, *they* had been in far greater peril than her.

'Ja'Prith's comrades were destroying every Corporation escape craft that tried to make a run for it back there. If he hadn't sent a mind-message to tell them your ship carried friends, not foes, they'd have knocked you out of the sky too.'

Talk of 'mind-messages' had provoked more questions. But Snow was reluctant to discuss her new-found abilities. She had not yet had time to come to terms with them herself.

Now the others were back on board the vessel, preparing it for the start of its journey back to Earth.

But Snow was finding it difficult to leave.

🔅 🌱 ⚗ ● ◉ Ⓐ ⬦ ⬡ ◉ ⬢

She had only known her father's mind-mate for a short space of time, but the bond between them was already remarkably strong. Telepathic connections ran deep, she was beginning to realize. And there was still so much she wanted to ask about her father.

A sudden desperate thought flashed into Snow's mind – triggering an instant response from Ja'Prith.

*No. You should not stay.*

The giant creature turned his elongated head to look at the columns of fire and smoke rising from the research centre in the distance.

*Look!* urged Ja'Prith's mind-voice. *The Corporation is finished here. Kasteesh is free once more. I and my brothers and sisters will labour to return our great city to its former glory. The Chairman will not chain us again!*

The creature turned his gaze back to Snow.

*To see out my days with you in your father's place, on my back, would thrill my heart. But your home world has great need of your unique powers. It is up to you and your order to fight the Corporation's evil at its heart – on Earth.*

Snow hung her head. The voice in her mind

became more tender.

*For many cycles I have lived in the hope that Hoshiko was only beyond the range of my thoughts, not beyond the grave. But I am at peace now. Your father may no longer survive in body, but his spirit lives in you, brave Alida.*

*You have rescued me from a prison cell. And you have freed me from something far worse – my grief. For both, I am for ever in your debt.*

Ja'Prith bowed his alien head low to the ground, in a gesture of respect. When he lifted it again, his eyes were sparkling.

*I look forward to the next time we fly together, daughter of Hoshiko.*

Sensing that this was his parting thought, Snow forced a smile and formed her own farewell mind-message.

*As do I. Take care, Ja'Prith.*

She watched as the noble creature extended his huge wings and launched himself powerfully into the air.

Before long, he was a dark speck against the sky, then gone altogether.

Snow turned and made her way slowly up the freighter's boarding ramp.

✷ ⚘ ⧋ ◉ ⊡ ⒜ ⬯ ⬠ ◎ ⬡

Salt's desire to make a swift departure was understandable. Their four-day time limit – the period over which they were supposedly visiting the out-of-town smelting plant – was fast running out. Time was of the essence.

Although the freight ship had a stardrive and would serve to get them home, it would take time to manoeuvre the sluggish vessel out of Kasteesh's orbit before they could safely make the spatial jump.

Then there was more time to allow for the tricky last stage of their journey, once back on Earth – their return to the Academy itself. Salt's plan was to ditch the freighter half a day's hike from the smelting complex, then make their way to the complex on foot. He was confident his friend Rajsim could arrange for them to return to Nu-Topia by shuttle – as though having completed their 'field trip' – without raising anyone's suspicions.

It was only after Salt had piloted the ship out of Kasteesh's atmosphere that Snow had an opportunity to speak to him privately. As the vessel thrummed its way steadily towards the point where they could safely engage its stardrive, she approached her old mentor, a little nervously. The others were busy goggling at the amazing views of the planet below – this was only their second experience of space travel and they had spent the whole of their first journey shut in a dark cargo pod.

'Master.' Snow tried her best not to sound accusing. 'Why did you never tell me the truth about my parents?'

Salt hit a flashing control button, then turned slowly in his pilot's chair to give Snow his full attention. The gruff old armourer's eyes shone with uncharacteristic tenderness.

'I'm sorry for being less than honest with you,

believe me,' he rumbled. 'I gave your father my word. I hope you can forgive me.'

Snow nodded silently.

'If there is anything you wish to know about your parents, I will be do my best to answer any questions,' continued Salt. 'I have honoured my promise. Now is no longer the time for half-truths.'

Snow looked down for a moment, then lifted her gaze to meet his. 'Then . . . what really happened to them?'

Salt drew a long, slow breath. 'You were less than four months old when your father brought you to me,' he began. 'At the Academy, under cover of night. We had never met before, but Hoshiko had sought me out as a fellow Armouron – the only person he believed he could trust.

'He told me of his life with the Mshanga; of his capture by the Corporation; and of the torment he suffered at their hands – but I imagine your friend Ja'Prith has already recounted that part of your father's tale?'

Snow nodded. 'But Ja'Prith never knew what happened to him after he was taken to Earth,' she said quietly.

'He escaped,' said Salt. 'He wanted dearly to return to Kasteesh to free Ja'Prith – he suffered greatly from their separation. But he was terrified of falling into the Corporation's hands again. Not because he feared for his own life, you understand. He was no coward. But he realized that the advanced mental powers he was developing were something the Chairman would do anything to duplicate – so that he could use them for his own corrupt ends.

'So your father went into hiding. The White Knights sought him relentlessly. For some time, he managed to evade them. He even met and fell in love with your mother. You were born two years after his escape. But only months later, his luck ran out. The Corporation located your family home somehow. A team of White Knights staged a night raid. Your father only just managed to get you away safely.'

'My mother?' pressed Snow.

'She was killed in the attack on your home,' Salt said gently. 'Your father was a broken man when he left you in my care. That night in the Old School, he made me swear two things: to do everything in my power to keep you safe; and that when you were old enough to ask after him, I should tell you he was dead. He feared that otherwise you would attempt to seek him out and put yourself in danger. And he was quite certain that his death was imminent. He left his medallion with me – the one which you now bear in your breastplate. An Armouron Knight only surrenders their medallion on their deathbed.'

Salt reached out to take one of Snow's neat hands in his own massive palm.

'I spent only a few hours in your father's company. But it was enough to recognize him as a brave, noble man. He would be as proud of what you achieved back there on Kasteesh as I am.' He smiled warmly. 'You have the same fearless spirit I saw in your father that night.'

*His spirit lives in you.*

Snow suppressed a sudden swell of emotions as she recalled Ja'Prith's farewell.

'Thank you, master,' she said simply. 'I just needed to know.'

She turned away and crossed slowly to one of the large viewports in the ship's side. She stared blankly out at the shrinking sphere of Kasteesh.

She knew that she, like Ja'Prith, must seek to

accept her father's death. But her adventure on Kasteesh had brought buried feelings of loss to the surface again. All too briefly, it had seemed that her heart's desire – that her parents would someday miraculously return to her life – had been about to come true.

She must recognize that desire for the fantasy it was and let it go. She must find a way to be at peace with her father's death, as his beloved mind-mate had done.

But it was hard.

# Epilogue

Parqul-Tuz moved a claw over his air-chair's steering sensor, causing it to rotate ninety degrees.

'You see those?'

The Auroxilan extended one of his several stubby arms to point at a row of a dozen wagons standing near the brink of the vast salt quarry of which he was owner and boss.

The white-haired stranger nodded silently.

'They're full of salt-rock,' continued Tuz. 'The whole lot needs splitting down for processing.'

He looked back at the human.

'The day-shift splitters signed off an hour ago. I'm short of somebody to work nights. The job's yours if you start immediately. All the tools you'll need are in the wagon with the tarpaulin over it.'

He fixed the man with a hard three-eyed stare.

'I'll pay fifty credits for every wagon-load you split. If you're as strong as you say, you should get through a couple a night. Interested?'

The human eyed the row of wagons for a few moments before replying.

'If you double the rate, I will do them all tonight.'

Tuz snorted incredulously. His flabby blue body began to shake with laughter.

'*All* of them! Don't be a fool! There isn't a being in the galaxy who could split twelve wagons of salt-rock in a single eight-hour shift!'

But the human's earnest expression didn't falter. He was serious.

Tuz gave another snort. He sensed a chance to profit from the stranger's foolishness.

'Fine – double-pay if you manage all of them. But *half*-pay if you don't. What do you say to that?'

The man paused briefly before nodding again.

'You've got yourself a deal!' roared Tuz. 'And good luck with achieving the impossible!'

He turned his air-chair and glided away, still chortling to himself about the human's ludicrous proposition.

Once alone, the man strode purposefully towards the first wagon.

'Nothing is impossible,' he murmured to himself, 'if you put your mind to it . . .'

Standing before the wagon, he closed his eyes. His brow furrowed and a look of intense concentration filled his face.

Four massive rocks on top of the first piled wagon began to rise slowly into the air. They floated up, then across, to hover impossibly over a part-filled crate of split rock. There was a series of loud *cra-ack* sounds and neat fractures suddenly appeared in each of the levitating rocks. Their fragments tumbled down into the crate.

The man immediately focused his concentration on the next layer of rocks. He had a hard night's work ahead of him. But it was worth it. On the terms he had agreed, the pay would be enough to begin his journey back to Earth.

And he *had* to get back – whatever it took and whatever the risk. There was someone he was desperate to see.

Someone he would happily cross a galaxy for . . .